Bonny,

Thank you for supporting my writing!

The Face Maker

and other stories of obsession

JOE PONEPINTO

Woodward Press

Copyright © 2013 by Joe Ponepinto

Woodward Press, LLC, a Limited Liability Company
48929 Sugarbush
Chesterfield MI 48047

woodwardpress.com

All rights reserved. No part of this publication may be reproduced or transmitted in any form or by any means, electronic or mechanical, including photocopy, recording, or any information storage and retrieval system, without permission in writing from the publisher.

For information about permission to reproduce selections from this book, contact the Publisher by email at permissions@woodwardpress.com.

ISBN-13: 978-0-9838261-2-5

For all the broken faces

About the Cover:

WWI soldier facial reconstruction casts and masks created by Anna Coleman Ladd, ca. 1918 / American Red Cross, photographer. Anna Coleman Ladd papers, Archives of American Art, Smithsonian Institution.

Used by permission of the Archives of American Art at the Smithsonian Institution in Washington D.C.

The image is of the artisan's workshop, taken at Place de la Concorde, ca. 1918. The photo is a silver gelatin print, measuring 12 x 17 cm.

World War I (known then as The Great War), was one of the first conflicts fought with modern weapons, however, the tactics employed by armies had not changed since the days of single-shot muskets. This resulted in millions of traumatic injuries, especially facial disfigurements, of which thousands of men suffered. Since plastic surgery was in its infancy at the time, artists stepped in to design faces to cover the war wounds, and give the soldiers some semblance of their pre-war appearance. They worked from photos taken before the injuries, and matched facial features, in many cases creating façades that could not be detected unless the viewer was close up. Plaster, metal and other materials were used to create the masks.

For an extensive article on World War I facial injuries and the efforts to repair them, please see http://www.smithsonianmag.com/history-archaeology/mask.html.

Contents

The Face Maker *originally published in Midwest Literary Magazine*	1
The Killer of the Writer *originally published in The Lifted Brow*	19
Living in Dark Houses *originally published in Fiction Fix*	37
The Sting of the Glove *originally published in The Apalachee Review*	53
Nixon in State *originally published in Lumina*	69
Caging the Butterfly	85
Excerpts from the Diary of the Last Roman Emperor	101
What We Choose to Remember	115
Minutiae (Author's Notes)	137

The Face Maker

The soldier is a client, not a patient, yet Alistair Leeds cares more for him than any of the doctors who worked on the case. The surgeons did what they could—removed the shards of pulverized bone from the side of his face, cauterized the ravaged flesh, stitched him back together roughly, like a cheap blanket. They saved the man's life, if exile can be considered a life, because with his monster's visage he can never participate in the world as he once had. A mortar shell has taken that from him. It's stolen the exchanges with friends, the moments that define a man and need a face to express them: a smile when a pretty girl passes by, contentment when the sun breaks through fog, fascination at the headlines in a news rack. All that is forbidden now, lost in deference to the sensitivities of the crowd, who would be horrified should he expose this consequence of battle to them. They prefer to think of the war as a glorious struggle, from which their heroes came back whole, or not at all, and this human gargoyle in their midst would be too great a dose of truth, too terrible for them to bear.

Leeds will give him his life back. He has worked for weeks to prepare the remedy, relying on art, not medicine. In the early evening dim of his studio he lifts a thin cast from its tray by an edge and holds it in his palm. He stands in shadow and bathes it in the glow of a single bulb—it is as beautiful as a sculpture by Rodin, as beautiful even as God's design. A simple pat of clay, given life by the artist's imagination, fashioned to cure what the surgeons could not, and salve the wounds that religion cannot comfort.

The client, a corporal, waits, not daring to believe. He sits on the edge of a table in the workshop, his raw and monstrous features uncovered now that he has the safety of closed doors. His wife stands with him. The shroud he wore outside hangs from his hand, still ready to cover his shame.

The client is the twelfth Leeds has seen this month, more than he treated in the first three quarters of 1918. The lads are coming home from the war by the thousands now, many shot through with bullets and shrapnel, missing arms or legs, some with their lungs burned away by mustard gas, others having lost their wits from shell shock. At least the Armistice means this parade of unfortunates will soon end. Those with savaged faces are Leeds's specialty, and he has been preparing small masks to cover their mutilations ever since the government admitted it was incapable of easing their misery. And in treating the symptoms of the carnage he has found a way to be useful, more useful than with the uninspired slabs he tried to pass off as sculpture, or the mottled canvases that were his paintings before the war. The degree he received at university has some meaning now.

This client bears remarkable disfigurement. When he first came in Leeds peered closely, despite the soldier's reluctance, to inspect the abuses wrought by combat. He had become something of an expert on facial anatomy through his craft, if only through the sheer number of clients sent his way as the Great War wound down. He took meticulous notes, like a doctor, to catalog the injuries. Half the mandible missing, he wrote in his book; the remains of the masseter muscle receded into a chasm below the palate. Maxilla and zygomatic bones largely missing too; zygomaticus major and minor severed. But the medical terms obscured the truth, kept him from seeing the real damage, from feeling the man's anguish over the dashing soldier he had been and the ogre he was now condemned to be. The soldier sighed, breaking Leeds's concentration. Leeds stopped his note taking and looked at his client then as he should have, as one man to another, registering the crushed eye and the pink flap of skin that looked as though someone had boiled it. Leeds saw pain in every movement, pain in the man's realization that he would remain trapped in this freakish shell for the rest of his life.

Clearly the experts hadn't spent much time trying to save this man's face, had considered it hopeless and moved on to other, more salvageable, patients. The evidence of their clumsy ministrations surrounded the wounds. Seared bits of flesh clung to the edges of the damage, clues to their primitive science. What torture did they use on this man, Leeds wondered. A blowtorch? A branding iron?

"Passchendaele," the soldier explained, as if that were all that needed to be said. "One of my chums, sir," he went on, his speech a slur of spit and effort. "He told me you might help."

The Belgian quagmire. Three-quarters of a million men slaughtered. Leeds could not stop looking at the blistered wound. "You poor soul," he said. "What happened over there?"

The soldier looked away from him. "A nightmare. It went on for months. Death everywhere. The only way to understand was to be there."

"I wish I could have."

"Stationed back here, eh? You're a lucky chap, sir."

"No. I wasn't in the army."

"Didn't you join up?"

"I wanted to. I almost did." Leeds continued looking at the

soldier's face. This could have happened to him. Maybe it should have. He pushed his hair—his long, civilian hair—out of his eyes, and considered turning the man away. The task was probably too great to attempt anyway. Leeds had designed noses and jaws, cheekbones and even a row of teeth, but nothing on this scale. Better to send him to another artist, someone with more experience. But the mutilation was so great, perhaps no one else would be willing to help him. He looked once more at the soldier, sitting straight, as though at attention, waiting for Leeds to deliver his verdict, and ready to follow the orders no matter what they might entail. "I will do what I can," Leeds said.

"Yes, sir," the soldier said.

In the days that followed Leeds took photographs and made sketches from several angles. He took dozens of measurements and re-measurements from the right side of the face—the exact distance from the bridge of the nose to the cheek, from the lower eyelid to the corner of the mouth—so that he might construct a complement to the healthy side. And when he finished he altered the numbers just slightly, because no one's face is a mirror from side to side. Variations and flaws set one hemisphere off from the other, and in those discrepancies a man's character begins to be revealed. An artist would know that. In talking to the soldier over the course of the process he learned of his humor, his love of adventure, and from this he knew which way to change the readings—he would make this side of the face just slightly more pleasant than the other, more eager to smile, to show the soul of the man behind the ghoul's visage.

In his shop, at night, working under the flickering bulb, Leeds prepared the mask. He waited until his other tasks of the day were done before beginning, moving noses and cheeks and bits of hard skin prepared for his other clients out of view, in order to give the soldier's face his complete focus. Still, the first four attempts that week produced disasters and had to be discarded—the molds refused to take the shape he'd imagined, and when the ceramic cooled he saw instantly how they would insult the client. One would have given him a protruding chin, like a Habsburg; another would have made his cheekbones so uneven he might appear to have a defect. Had he not been so serious about his task, Leeds might have laughed at his failures.

The fifth try came closer. He pulled the naked material from the cast and held it next to the photographs. He turned it to match the views in the sketches, and saw that it was nearly right—just a little more bulge to the cheek, a slight roundness at the point of the jaw would make it correct. He became excited and ignored that midnight had passed, and set to work again on the mold while the kiln came up to temperature. This man, this soldier would have a face again. He would give it to him. Near dawn he fired the sculpture. While it cooled, the sun rose and he slept.

He dreamt of faces, as he often does now. People from Oxford Street, near his London shop, those he knew from stores and pubs, but made grotesque, their features contorted in torture; and military officers who'd had their eyes gouged out, flailing their arms in the darkness and barking orders at him to restore their sight. He tried, as in every one of these nightmares, to tell them he lacked the skill, but he could not speak, and they marched on him like a platoon of the dead until he woke. It's a product of this unpleasant job, he told himself as he removed the nightshirt soaked with sweat. It will pass when the last of the clients has been served.

The remainder of that morning and most of the afternoon he spent with the brushes. Leeds removed his spectacles and bent to within a few inches of the ceramic, as though painting a miniature portrait. He used his finest round, detailing the mask point by point, creating a face from a mosaic of droplets, making the skin come alive with nuance, hinting at veins beneath the surface, adding the shadow of a beard, reproducing every pore. He paused often, closing his eyes to remember the precise coloring of the soldier's face. Perhaps he should have the man here, posing so he could match each hue exactly, but no, not necessary. Leeds remembered it all. His empathy for the man's condition made the memory as real as if he sat in front of him.

Their schedule called for the soldier to return the next day, and Leeds believed the results would please him. He had never created anything so lifelike, so well suited to the task. A better match than a photograph. Content, he thought to go back to his other jobs, to catch up on the work he'd ignored for the past week. But not yet. He needed one more look at this marvel he had created.

Touching only the edges he lifted the mask from its cradle of gauze, and held it at arm's length. Flawless. It would cover the wounds, and from a distance no one could tell the man had ever suffered injury. Leeds smiled—now the soldier would have to wear his medals in public so people knew he had served in the war. Of course up close the tragedy would be obvious. The soldier could speak, but only one side of his mouth would move. Only half of him could show anger or gladness, or any emotion at all. He would just have to live with it, as would Leeds. Like his other attempts at art, it didn't quite work—it wasn't right, not what he had originally intended. The left side of the man's face would be a statue, a rigid memory of a single moment from his life—a moment now lost and plastered over with the artist's good intentions—a façade, a counterfeit, worse even than the pieces he had exhibited in the local gallery. He remembered his disappointment when the critic from the Times called his efforts pretentious, the self-deluding work of an amateur. This mask was sham art too—nothing more than cold, lifeless clay, as immobile as what it would replace. Less horrifying than the injuries, but still no cure for the soldier's condition. There would be little difference between the pain of his disfigurement and the embarrassment of this charade covering his face.

How Leeds had fooled himself into believing he had discovered an answer. How he had let his ego deceive him—the same false superiority that let him believe he had a future as an artist, that kept him from enlisting during the war because he was too valuable a talent. It had concealed the real reason he did not fight—what he had hidden—his cowardice. Each time he thought of himself in the trenches he saw his death. He would line up along the wall with the other soldiers. A captain would give the command, and up they would go, into the craters and barbed wire of No Man's Land and certain annihilation.

No, the mask was as flawed as the soldier's ravaged skin. To place it on his face would be a crime. A hero of the nation deserved better.

Leeds threw the ceramic to the floor and it came apart in a dozen pieces. He ran to the telephone and cranked up the operator, and had her patch him through. "Don't come," he begged the soldier. "Not tomorrow. I need more time."

"Not tomorrow?" the soldier asked.

"Please. It's not good enough. I can make it better."

"How long, then?"

"A few more days. Maybe a week."

"Well... I see. Another week."

"I am trying. I want you to know that. It's not as though I haven't been trying." Leeds could hear the man stifling his emotions. He thought he heard him fighting to keep from crying, holding back his agony over his deformities. "I'm sorry," he said.

There was a pause. Finally the soldier said, "It's alright, sir. I've waited so long. A few more days won't make a difference."

Leeds's thanks were profuse.

"No, sir," the soldier said. "Thank you. Thank you for everything you're doing to help me."

But how to do it? How to make it lifelike, real? To begin, the mask must be made flexible, so that when the soldier moved the good side of his face, the other would move with it and create the impression of animation. To do so it would have to expand and contract, like an elastic. Leeds felt the side of his own face, the tension in the skin, the pliability—bands of muscle connecting bones, covered with skin that stretched and tightened with every motion. It was that simple. Clearly the ceramic he'd been using to fashion the mask represented only part of the answer—it could give the face its essential shape and underlying structure, it could fill in what the mortar had taken away, but it couldn't be the sole material. He would have to marry its hardness to something softer.

Leather was skin—or it once was. Perhaps a thin layer of leather, or something like it, could be dyed to the color of the soldier's flesh and bonded to a ceramic base. Leeds cut strips of cowhide from a pair of gloves, and spent the better part of the next day changing their color and thickness—a wasted day, however. The leather, having already been processed, had given up its elasticity at the tannery. He should have known. It was a stupid mistake—another in what had become a series of errors—and soon he would have to tell the soldier that his ineptitude, his lack of talent as an artist was insufficient. He should never have agreed to help this man. The job hovered beyond him, and he should have known it from the start, but he'd let his ego talk him into it. Soon, everyone would know what a fraud he was.

He took the work of the past few days and threw it into the stove. Sparks shot up as the pieces dislodged the burning coal, and lit the anger inside him. Leeds swept his chisels and scrapers from his worktable onto the floor. "A failure!" he raged. "I am a charlatan! I am not an artist." He took his sculptor's mallet and flung it, blindly, and it smashed through the shop's window and onto the sidewalk outside. Winter air began streaming through the jagged glass, and halted his tantrum. He realized even this childish display was just another act in the impostor's performance: the suffering artist wrestling his emotions on the way to achieving fame. What utter nonsense.

He plugged the hole with a wall of clay, but in the time it had taken to repair the damage, the temperature in the shop had dropped at least fifteen degrees. The ceramics he'd placed in the stove had melted over the coals, snuffing the fire, which added to the chill. But Leeds did nothing to rekindle the flame. He curled up on the floor, next to the last vestige of heat from the stove, and willed himself to sleep.

He awoke—frigid, shivering—wrapped around the base of icy metal, his breath mimicking the London fog. It took several minutes to convince his body to function well enough so he could pour new coal into the belly and light it. When he finally had a sustained flame, he huddled next to the stove until the heat became too intense to bear, inducing a sweat, and reminding him he had not washed at all during the days of his obsession over the mask. Now he repulsed himself physically as well as mentally. He clawed at his clothes, ripping the buttons from his shirt to get it off, tearing his pants as he struggled with them, removing everything until he stood naked in the heat of the shop, daring pedestrians to see him through the broken window.

As he leaned into the washbasin to splash himself, he began, at last, to calm. His breathing slowed. His skin cooled, and he relaxed as he dabbed himself with a towel. There were some fresh garments in a drawer next to his bed, and Leeds laid them across the sheets. When he had dried, he would slip them on and think of what he might do with the rest of his life—he could sell the shop and the implements, perhaps find a position with the brokerage house where his uncle worked. Or he could travel for a time. With the war over, steamer lines would be desperate for customers, and passage would be cheap. He could go to places the war had hardly touched—Sweden and Norway, or south, around the Spanish coast to southern Italy, maybe Sicily. He could live without the constant reminders of the last four years, of his failures and his cowardice. And there, wherever he found himself, he could decide how to spend his days. At least he knew the charade of being an artist, and the madness that had come with it, had ended.

A ray of sun parsed the canopy that stifled London in winter. A good sign. It made the shop bright enough that Leeds could shave by its light, and he brought the bowl and straight razor into the middle of the workspace so he could enjoy the glow while he cleaned himself. After all those days fixated on the soldier's face, he had grown haggard, and despite letting the lather sit on his skin for a few minutes he found the shave difficult. The dull blade tugged and caught with each stroke. He knew if he maintained that pressure he'd eventually nick himself, but he couldn't stop. He wanted to get on with his new life, quickly, and instead of stopping and sharpening the razor, he continued to drag it over his neck until he sliced a good piece of skin.

The wound gushed, blood streaming over his Adam's apple and down his chest. He wet a towel to staunch it and it stung, as though he'd squeezed citrus into the cut. It took several minutes to get the bleeding to subside, and when it finally did, when he wiped the last trickle of blood from his neck, Leeds saw a small patch of skin hanging under his jaw. It must be dead already, because it no longer hurt. Without thinking, he pulled it away from his neck and sliced it free, reopening the wound. But the fresh flow of blood and pain did not interest him.

Leeds put the blade down and brought the patch close for examination. He took the ends between his fingers and pulled. He rolled the bit of skin against the palm of his hand. Fleshy and firm, as if it were still alive, still part of him. It gave when he flattened it, sprang back when he released. He turned towards the sun, now visible over the roofs of the buildings across the street. His eyes widened. What is more like skin than skin?

The blood continued to fall from his neck, and Leeds held the towel against the flow. When he pressed with force it stopped long enough for him to explore further with the razor. The point of the blade, where it smoothed into the curve of the spine, was sharp even if the rest of the edge was not, and Leeds used it like a surgeon to probe, to slip between the layers of epidermis and pry them apart. It was not enough for his fingers to take hold, but it was enough for him to see that the solution to the soldier's misery had been right in front of him all along.

A whetstone—he had one somewhere among the sculptor's tools—and with one hand holding the towel against the blood, Leeds rummaged through the mess he'd made last night when he had nearly lost belief in himself. He'd been ready to give up his art, his livelihood, the steady march towards artistic acceptance and success. This must have been God's way of testing him, of showing him the path to take, and he sat on the floor of the shop with the stone between his legs, raking the blade back and forth over its grit, until it was keen enough to continue.

No one had seen so far—perhaps the unseasonable sun had made a mirror of the shop window—but Leeds drew the curtains now just the same. He stood back from the shaving glass and examined his nude form. The skin covering the stomach was the smoothest and softest, and offered the greatest in surface area, but the inner thighs were ripe as well. So too, the underside of the arms, the portion from the biceps to the triceps that lays against the torso. All of it was approximately the right texture. He was glad he was not as hairy as other men. He moved to the glass and positioned the razor to begin.

The first touch was a pinprick. Leeds drew the blade sideways across his abdomen, barely pressing the spine, letting the edge slip through the first layer of skin but no deeper. It drew no blood, only a transparent strip curling backwards from his flesh. He made another pass, gently, until the sheet of skin grew large enough to grasp with tweezers. Then he pulled and cut simultaneously, etching a patch from his belly. His subsequent slices were not as deft as the first, and at least half the time he tapped the capillaries, drawing trickles of blood. It hurt, but not enough to stop. Fear that he might injure himself, in fact, was greater than the pain, but he controlled it—a simple matter of priorities: the welfare of the brave soldier, his duty to the wounded men, his own resurrection as an artist—they far outweighed any discomfort he might experience. In time the singe of pain that accompanied each incision became encouragement. Each carried a jolt of electricity, recharging his spirit, cleansing him of past sins. Before the hour was up he had collected a small pile of scraps on the worktable. The skin where he had flensed himself was beet-like, raw and fleshy, filled with glowing corpuscles working to repair the damage. The excised pieces resembled a book of parchment that had lost its binding, like an old Bible come undone. And like those ancient pages the skin would soon dry out if he didn't protect it. Leeds wrapped the pieces in the same moist fabric he used to store his clay. He remembered a humidor his father had given him one Christmas in hopes he would learn to enjoy a good cigar. He'd never pursued the habit, but he'd kept the box, and now it would enjoy a better, fuller purpose.

Again to the mirror. The amount of skin he'd peeled so far scarcely yielded enough to cover an eyelid—he would have to harvest much more to give the mask the depth and feel of a real face, and to hide the huge area left bare by the war. Leeds turned his attention to his legs. He sat on the floor and buried his head between his knees, where he could work with the focus and precision needed to make the delicate cuts. More and more skin added to the collection; more raw flesh exposed to the burning air. Despite his meticulous incisions, however, he was losing blood, a trickle at a time, but still enough to stain much of his body a rusty brown as it dried. With each drop he felt weaker, but forced himself to hang on until he believed he had enough material to cover the mask, and had it stored away, properly. Only then did Leeds allow himself to lurch towards the bed in the back of the shop. Perhaps night had fallen, perhaps not. He had failed to notice whether the day had passed. His skin continued to sing as he slept, and he twitched unconsciously from the discomfort—but his nightmares, the faces that had plagued him since he'd begun this work, were gone. He dreamed a peaceful scene in which he flew, like an eagle over the city, searching for a place to land.

But he had slept without clothes. He woke coughing and congested, in the grip of fever. He could not bathe in that condition—the sting of water would be too painful and might add to his malaise—so he threw the bed's comforter over him, like a shroud, and set to work again. The mold for the last mask had been correct, and he began there by carefully sanding the surfaces to reduce them and increase their grip on the adhesive that would hold the skin in place. Back and forth he went to the photographs and measurements he had taken, carefully configuring the base of the mask to act as bone, to fill, exactly, the canyons of the soldier's face excavated by the war. Each motion burned his pulsing flesh and joints. His head pounded and swooned with sickness. He could not focus on the tasks in front of him, but he refused to abandon them.

Leeds took the gossamer of his skin out of the box, piece by piece, and laid the layers on top of each other, kneading them gently with his fingers, adding hints of calendula oil for moisture, pressing them down with a roller. To his surprise they displayed memory—they bonded to each other as though reforming the organ that once enveloped his body. He massaged the mass until it became a single portion of skin, rolled it out, then balled it again and started over, continuing to work it into the proper shape. Again, the hours passed, but Leeds was oblivious to time, or to the need to eat or drink, to rest or even to stop for a moment to wipe his brow and reflect. He was an artist now, living apart from the universe of incompetence in which he had been trapped, and existed in a place of his own making, a place in which the limitations of that other world no longer applied.

Once the skin had been formed to fit over the base, he attached it with a permanent adhesive, a strong glue used in construction. A drop to attach at the sphenoid bone, another at the zygomatic, and one at the maxilla. The edge of the skin attached along the jaw, connecting at the mandible. He clamped them all into place and let the assembly sit in its gauze on the worktable. Leeds noticed it had become dark again, but he could not bring himself to sleep, and he sat, tented in the bedcover, watching the assembly until morning. He did not want to touch it, but as it was to be worn and used, and would have to handle weather, he knew he had to test to ensure it could stand up to the stresses of daily life. As the fresh light of day came through the shop window Leeds removed the clamps and held his creation in the sun—it seemed beautiful. But still… something was wrong.

He had cheated. Yes, the skin was real, but was it true? Was this the creation of an artist, the product of a man who had given his soul in creation?

He did not ponder his next decision. He would act on the impulse, because action, not thought, is what matters. It is what wins wars. The razor felt cool and substantial in his hand. He had practiced enough on the rest of his body, and there was no hesitation now as he brought the knife's edge to his cheek, just below the eye, and described a furrow, not a millimeter deep, back almost to his ear, down and around, tracing the jawline, and back up, behind the lips to where he started. The soldier's face would be real now, and Leeds took hold of the flap of skin he had etched and pulled it away from the layer underneath in a single stroke, a single rip that bared his soul, and caused pain so great that at last he cried out, "My God!

When will my penance be done?" He fell to a knee, still clutching the fresh skin. With his last reserve of will, Leeds crawled to his table and laid it over the top of the mask, holding it there, willing it to fuse with the skin that had already bonded.

Three days passed before he woke again. He could feel his body emaciated from lack of food and water, and covered with scabs where the wounds he inflicted were just beginning to heal. His face felt taut and sore. His forehead pulled towards his chin, and he could scarcely open his left eye. He struggled to the table and examined his work. He went to the telephone and turned the crank.

The soldier squints while Leeds stands in shadow, turned to the side with his hair covering half his face.
"You don't have to be afraid," Leeds says to him.
The soldier sits on the edge of the table and drops the blanket to the floor. He shies away from Leeds, still embarrassed, and takes his wife's hand.
"Turn to the right," Leeds says. His voice is a rasp. He slips the mask into place over the wound and applies a touch of spirit gum to secure it. After a minute to let it set, he tests: "Open your mouth," he commands.
The soldier looks confused.
"Please do. I need to check the fit."
The new skin stretches with the old. When he closes his mouth it retracts.
"Speak to me. What was your regiment?"
"Royal Fusiliers."
"When did you join?"
"March, 1915."
Leeds sees the mask move as naturally as the skin of a man who has never experienced a moment of pain.

"Can you smile for me?"

It is a grimace more than a smile, but what could Leeds expect from a man who has been through what this corporal has.

The soldier reaches to touch his new face. When his fingers meet the skin they pull away, amazed at the sensation. He touches again, caressing the artwork, as though probing for meaning. His wife turns to him and holds his face in her hands, and emits a gasp of surprise.

And when Leeds holds the little mirror before the man so he can see for himself, the soldier cries. From his undamaged eye a tear forms and hoists itself over the rim of his lower lid, and Leeds thinks it is much like the lads lifting themselves over the berms of their trenches, going over the top, into the abyss and the meat grinder of the German machine guns. The tear washes down the corporal's good cheek and holds at the base of his chin, as though waiting for gravity to muster the strength to pull it free. To his credit, the man does not sob or lose composure, and Leeds turns away momentarily, pretending to search for a tool, to give the poor soldier a chance to regain his dignity.

"Dear God," the soldier's wife says. "What has he done to you?"

No less than a miracle, Leeds wants to say, but it would be so immodest. Let the work speak for itself. The fact that the soldier can walk in public again is testament enough.

"I must make a few minor adjustments," Leeds says.

"No!" says the soldier. There is still a slur to his speech, but that will vanish as he becomes used to the feeling of the new skin.

"You have done enough," his wife says. She takes her husband's hand and leads him to the door. She whispers in his ear, and the only words Leeds can decipher are fragments of praise: "fixed," "trusted him," "a real doctor." He thinks he hears her say something about malpractice and finding a solicitor, but he obviously misheard.

Leeds says, "Please don't leave yet. There is still more to do."

"Thank you," the soldier says. "Thank you for trying, sir." And before Leeds can stop them they are outside, the wife again with her hands to his face, this time pulling at it, so enamored is she by its genius. When he looks again they are well down the sidewalk, walking briskly, the soldier a bit stooped, the wife with her arm around his shoulders.

He has done good work today, negating a tiny part of the evil that plagued the continent for four years. A pity they did not stay and let him complete the last few manipulations. Still, the mask is perfect, so much better than a mere piece of ceramic. What pulls at Leeds, however, almost angers him, is that there are thousands of men just like this client, used and discarded like matchsticks. He must contact all those for whom he has made masks and tell them to come back in—he can do for them what he has done for the soldier.

In time, though. It will take a few weeks for him to recover from the ordeal of this project. Next time it will go more efficiently, now that he has experience, now that he understands. He realizes he has been working so hard he hasn't been out of the shop for days—maybe weeks. Leeds peers out from behind the curtains to the street and for a few minutes he watches women dodder to and from the markets, and laborers stumble into pubs to meet friends. He wants to be out with them.

He limps to the door—his legs tremble—and opens it, surveying the city. The air outside pierces him with cold—the deepest part of winter seems to be coming early this year. Leeds grasps the soldier's blanket—left behind in their haste—in his tired fingers. The man will not need it anyway. He pulls it to his face and wraps it around the wounds he has inflicted on himself. The public doesn't want to see the price of war, not even this ancillary cost. The chafe of clothing against his flesh turns each motion into a chorus of injury that threatens to swell into agony, but he must go out, back into the world. The flannel slips a little, allowing the icy air to prick his face, and it stings like a thousand needles. Leeds clutches the doorframe to steady himself, and shuffles onto the sidewalk, into the wind.

The Killer of the Writer

Among the hundreds of mourners who honored the great man sat the one who had killed him, disguised in dark glasses, anxious to pay his respects but unsure if his attendance would be tolerated.

They might kill him too, if they knew he'd infiltrated the crowd.

Flowers and literati filled the cathedral. A television crew broadcast from outside, reporting that the author had not yet completed his latest novel and that his agent and publisher debated if anyone could finish it for him. They told the newsman they might publish the manuscript unfinished, with a note regarding his passing to explain the truncation to future readers. They described his death as untimely, a tragedy, and a great loss to literature.

Pagán had taken a seat in the back, next to a woman who mentioned she had edited an article of the man's more than a decade before, prior to the first of his bestsellers, when he taught at the community college. She knew then Stephan Lazlo would become famous. His prose, his ideas—he was a genius, she said.

Jonathan Pagán was a writer too, but he did not share this fact with the woman or with anyone. He stayed up late many nights, after his wife went to sleep, and composed on his laptop in the kitchen, so he would not disturb her.

He sat very still throughout the service, clinging to the praise of the eulogists, absorbing their lovely words, and those passages of the author's works read by his friends, his former students, and his little grandson. Each of them stood at a podium set up in front of the open casket, the boy on a step to allow the audience to see him. None of them turned around to look at the body while they read. A colleague quoted from a work of Lazlo's that had won a Man Booker. The grandson read a letter that Lazlo had written to him for his last birthday. Some people in the rows in front of Pagán cried.

Jonathan Pagán was not a writer. He worked in a restaurant, as the night manager. The closest he ever came to writing in his job was updating the menus. He often added clever descriptions below the names of dinner items, which many of the customers found entertaining. For the andouille sausage and gumbo he wrote: "This dish is made from ingredients so rare, even we don't have them." It embarrassed him that he'd written it—especially to remember during the service.

"And how did you know him?" the woman asked.

"I didn't," Pagán said. He had not read any of Lazlo's books. The woman looked as though she would ask why, then, had he come, but the archbishop began his own remembrance, and Pagán ignored her and listened to the speech. Several mourners turned and stared at his dark glasses. Perhaps they thought him disrespectful, and what could he do except put his head down? If anyone asked directly, he would say he had an eye condition he didn't wish to expose. Eventually the people ignored him.

The loss of the writer encompassed more than mere emotion

inside the cathedral—it took on physical qualities, as though its dimensions could be measured by the number of people jammed into the pews, or the collective heft of their synchronous exhalations of grief. Of course, it rained that day.

Pagán waited until the service ended and went outside to watch the pallbearers place the casket in the hearse. Six men balanced the coffin on their shoulders, without using their hands to keep it steady. He had seen that on television once, a broadcast of a state funeral somewhere. What if one of the men stumbled?

Pallbearers. Coffin. Hearse. Pagán considered the terms. It occurred that much of our end is described by words not used elsewhere, except in metaphor. Funeral. Cemetery. Death is kept separate. He had tried to write about this in his stories, but had not been satisfied with the results.

It had been an auto accident, more the author's fault than his, although he had been driving faster than the posted limit, technically speeding, but so was everyone else. Lazlo drifted across the highway median and Pagán simply couldn't get out of the way. Some of the author's fans had discovered his email address and wrote to him—angry messages that accused him of murder and promised revenge. They became so disturbing that he had to close his account. Yet a rumor had spread, reported in one of the newspapers, that the author had driven drunk. He had come from a party held in honor of another author. Several witnesses said the two men had words. Pagán did not mention this testimony to his wife, and when she heard of it, she became upset.

"Why did you keep it a secret?" she asked.

"Do those things make a difference to you? Did you think the accident was my fault?"

"It doesn't matter whose fault it was," she said. "A great writer is dead."

She was right, and in looking at it from her viewpoint, he

realized he bore responsibility for Lazlo's death. Had he not been there, at that place, at that time, the writer would be alive. Pagán was not criminally liable, but understood he would carry the weight of this like a prison sentence. Lazlo's life and words had touched perhaps ten million people, but now those words would fade from the collective consciousness, their power dispersed into oblivion.

Pagán considered what might have happened had events altered slightly, if the angle of impact moved a few degrees, or if the integrity of the cars had been different. Lazlo could be alive and healthy, still writing and producing works of literary acclaim. It might have been Pagán who was killed. Would Lazlo have joined the scraggle of acquaintances who stood in the cemetery's dark breeze to watch him go down into the hole?

The night after the service, Pagán rose after midnight and wrote about his coworkers:

Felipe chose saguaro. A stately growth, and tall, like him. He picked a spot near a boulder, away from the other plants, and kicked at the sand until a depression formed. His left foot fit snugly in the hollow. Then he pawed again, with his right, and brought the other foot alongside.

He spread his arms, his body describing a cross. Pleats developed in his skin, ridges filled with water saved from a season ago, enough to sustain him and the birds that sucked at the flat white flowers he would soon produce from his head. His elbows rotated until his fingers pointed to the empty sky. Then the spines—ten thousand needles advancing from his flesh. Touch them, experience the promise of pain.

Felipe's skin weathered into a thick, tough hide. He lifted his face to the sun.

Martha was next. She had seen the poppies once, like badges of gold against a field of alfalfa. They appeared after a strong rain but lasted for only a few days before becoming dormant again, perhaps for years.

I tried to warn her but she lay on the ground, becoming ever thinner, and stretched herself for hundreds of yards, until she covered a small rise. She was glorious, evolving into a carpet of blossoms so joyful I imagined I heard their voices.

Felipe had chosen permanence, Martha a profound, fleeting emotion. I was jealous of them both.

Pagán had never visited the desert, but to write about it seemed natural.

A week after the funeral, a reporter from the Times tracked him down at home, while his wife worked. The man seemed courteous and promised he would only ask a few questions. Not until he was in the house did Pagán realize he did not want the notoriety.

The reporter wanted to know how the public's disdain for him, for killing an icon, even if by accident, had affected his life.

Pagán said not much had changed, then realized he'd given the wrong answer. He quickly added that he felt sadder than usual. He was sorry about the incident, and despaired over the loss of one so great. The distance between himself and his wife had grown because of it, he said.

"It's ironic," the reporter said, "that the man involved in Lazlo's death had never read a word of his. It's an interesting angle."

"Would it have been any different if I knew his work?" Pagán asked. "He would still be dead. What would have changed?"

"Maybe nothing. Maybe everything. As I said, our readers may find it interesting."

"Lazlo was drinking and driving," Pagán said. "Does anyone talk about that?"

"Lazlo's indulgences were well known," the reporter said.

When the story ran the next day it portrayed Pagán as cold and ignorant, a bitter man who had no remorse for what had happened. After he read it, Pagán called the restaurant and quit his job. The owner demanded that he give at least a month's notice, but Pagán explained he could not wait. He was despondent, he said. He needed to get away, to discover the man he had killed. Then he wrote a note for his wife: "My dearest, do not ask where I am going, because I do not know myself. I only know that I must learn what has been lost in me, and try my best to replace it." He packed a few things, his laptop and an old printer, stuffed them into the trunk of his car, and left.

He drove aimlessly through the city's depressed neighborhoods for a half hour, thinking about the note he'd left for his wife and how he should have made it longer, with a more sincere apology. He should have written that he still loved her and that he promised to return soon. Why hadn't he done that? At least it might have given her some solace. Like this he appeared heartless, maybe calculating, deserving of her disdain. When they'd argued she seemed more concerned about the dead man than him. But now he understood the guilt she accused him of had already formed, and she had revealed it to him.

Pagán purchased all of Lazlo's books, moved into a room on the edge of the city, and began reading.

He read from Lazlo's first novel:

She was called hard-bitten, as if she had been attacked in her sleep one night by a giant insect or a bat and now sported a wound that would never heal, the festering sore exposed to the world's polluted, burning air, its sting motivating her, filling each day with a fog of severity that enveloped whomever she came in contact with: those mean and deserving of her wrath, but also the innocent, who only happened to have been in the way. There were reasons for her pain. They justified her. She carried them like papers in a briefcase, ready to be produced whenever the question of her rage was raised.

Still, men wanted her. All that toughness had chiseled away the façade that hides most women from the world. It left her raw and exposed, but honest.

He read day and night for four weeks until he had finished every one of the novels and stories the great man had published.

The motel squeezed into in the neighborhood in which Lazlo had once lived when he first came to the city, penniless, at the age of nineteen. Abandoned and vandalized buildings lined the street as they had then. The air smelled of crime. It was noisy too, filled with the sounds of people frustrated at their lot, and it occurred to Pagán that this was where Lazlo first began to write about the need for suffering in a life, for without it, how can anyone appreciate the good?

His stories spoke of the down and out, people at the margins who had dreams but little hope. One novel concerned the lives of workers at a warehouse, based on a business not far from Pagán's room. Each of the employees faced a personal challenge. Some overcame their troubles, others did not. At the end of the book, one of the characters stood at an open window five floors above the street and looked out. Pagán could not decide if the man jumped or not.

He wondered if Lazlo had actually worked there for a time to understand the characters and the world in which they lived. In reading the story it seemed as though he had.

After Pagán finished reading Lazlo's works, he put on his only suit and went to see the man's widow. He did not make an appointment, fearing that she wouldn't wish to see him, but showed up at their mansion unannounced instead. As he steered his rusting car into the exclusive neighborhood he nearly stopped and turned back. He had rarely been in such a place and felt afraid he would be pulled over. Each home was perhaps ten times the size of the apartment he and his wife had shared. Landscape artists had manicured each estate like museum grounds. Cypress trees and statuary framed curved driveways.

He parked in the street, despite the signs that forbade parking, because he could not bring himself to park at the man's house, and walked a hundred yards to the front door.

As he went up the polished steps he realized the folly of his visit. There might not be anyone home. Lazlo's widow had probably gone to stay with relatives for a while, to help her through the difficult time. If she was home, she might throw him out or call the police.

But she was there. She opened the door and faced him. She wore jeans and a tattered gray sweatshirt, as though planning to work in the garden.

"You are that man," she said. "The one in the newspaper."

"I've come to apologize."

"Why?"

She had tied her hair in a ponytail and wore lipstick that looked and smelled of strawberries. Pagán could hear the television, loud and tuned to a talk show, in another room. The woman did not appear to be in mourning, but perhaps she suffered in her own way. He fought against the words forming in his mouth, but he had to say them—for her, for himself. Someone had to be culpable.

"I killed him. I'm so sorry. I killed your husband."

"But you are not responsible."

"Then who is?" he asked.

Mrs. Lazlo backed away from the door and swung it open. "Why don't you come in?" she said.

The home was what he expected, what he would have commissioned if he were the famous writer: marble floors and walls with wainscoting; a curated display of fine art lining the rooms and corridors, like a gallery. Lazlo's success as a writer had paid for it all.

She led him into a living room and gestured towards a ceiling that soared to the top of the second floor, as if this might impress him. She said, "The newspaper says you disappeared. You left your wife and no one has heard from you since."

"I don't plan on going back to that life."

"That's so strange."

"I cannot clear my conscience over this."

"I don't think I can help you with that," Mrs. Lazlo said.

"I want to know more about him. I've read everything, but I am still confused. When did he write, in the morning or at night? And how? Was it longhand? Did he use a computer?"

"What good will it do you to know that?" she asked.

"I am a writer." A wave of shame washed over him as he said it. He was not a writer, not in this house, not in the presence of the man's memory.

"Those aren't the things you should know," she said.

"Then, what?"

She hesitated, pretending to wipe the dust off the figure of a dancer made of worked and painted steel.

"My husband was a cheat. In every way," she said.

"He cheated on you?"

"On everyone. Yes, he cheated on me. And he cheated on the women he cheated on me with. He cheated at cards. He cheated the government. He would lie to you even when the truth would have made no difference."

"He lived his fictions," Pagán said. "What writer doesn't wish to do that?"

"He cheated death…"

"But he is dead."

"…and didn't care who was hurt by it." She walked to a small bar in the adjoining room and poured herself a glass of white wine, but did not offer one to him. "You don't know how many people would have killed him if they had the chance, if they thought they could get away with it. Half the writers and editors he knew. Most of the critics in the city. Every cuckolded husband whose wife slept with him because of some pretty story. Then you came along—an accident. He expected death to come from someone he knew."

"Why are you telling me this?"

"Yours is not the only conscience that's troubled."

Pagán noticed there were no photographs in the room, or in the rest of the house that he had seen. Nothing to indicate marriage or family. The opposite of his own wife's displays of proud relatives, posed in their best clothes, the pictures in formation along the dining room shelves.

"Was he a happy man?" he asked. "At least content?"

"What do you think?" she said.

"I would like to talk to his friends, his associates."

She had already finished the wine and began pouring another. "Friends? Try to find one." She took out a pen and slip of paper. "Here," she said. "Talk to his agent."

The agent would not see him at first, and after two weeks and repeated rebuffs, Pagán called and said the reason for the visit was to show her another of Lazlo's manuscripts, found among files untouched for several years.

He brought a box to the agent's office that looked as though it contained enough pages for a novel. By this time he looked haggard. He had not shaved in weeks and had worn the same few sets of clothes over and over, never getting them cleaned. The agent, Kristine Li, sat behind a large desk piled high with papers and asked her assistant, a young man who looked like he might have been a graduate student, to sit in on the meeting. She sipped from a plastic bottle of water but did not offer Pagán anything to drink.

The agent eyed the box, but Pagán kept it in his lap.

"How did you come across this manuscript?" she asked.

"I know his wife."

"And your relationship to Stephan…?"

"We are both writers."

"Let me see it."

Pagán didn't move. "I have a few questions first," he said. "I need to understand what will happen with his work… for his wife's peace of mind, of course."

"Like what? She never had concerns before."

"How long have you been working with Lazlo?"

"Eight years," she said. She studied a note on her desk, as if to say he was not important enough for her full attention.

"Did you sleep with him?"

She looked up. "What kind of a question is that? Are you here to give me the manuscript or not?"

"It's important," Pagán said. "No trouble will come from telling the truth. I won't tell his wife, or anyone. It's just important for me to know."

"I don't have to answer that."

"Then I know that you did."

"How dare you…"

The assistant rose, but he was a thin, bookish man and Pagán had no fear of him. At most he would dial the police.

Pagán tucked the box under his arm and left the office. "This is not for you," he said. The agent admonished him about legalities and the certainty of a lawsuit should he try to publish the book through someone else. Pagán walked to the elevator without looking back.

He continued to write in the little room, mostly at night when the noise from the neighborhood reached its peak. Cars with loud engines raced along the street, people talked and argued in groups. Some sounds—a woman's scream and shouts in anger—made him think crimes were being committed right outside his motel.

All of them had made their selections and became one with the land—plants, rocks, the sheer cliff of a distant mesa. I watched as the sun reached its apogee to bake the terrain, encasing the world in waves of heat, like a transparent enamel, preserving the scene. Where was my part in this? Why had I waited so long to choose?

The pull of civilization had not affected my friends as it did me. I weighed the possibility of eternity against the temporal place from which I had come, and felt a part of me remained there. My existence flitted away on cheap desires, living in moments that were lost forever as soon as they occurred. I could not remember the details of that life, but I knew it shackled me.

They had given it up so easily, so ecstatically that it made me wonder if they ever cared for that world at all.

A coyote appeared from behind a large rock. It circled around my feet three times and sat, facing me. "Why not become a quail or a lark?" he said. "You would still have the freedom of movement. You could go to places the others can't, escape the blaze of the sun in the daytime and the chill at night."

"Go away, trickster," I said. "You wish me a bird so that you may eat my eggs and then eat me. I should become an eagle, then we'll see who eats whom."

The idea of soaring over the desert valley appealed to me, drifting on thermals and nesting in the rocks. I spread my arms and imagined them wings. My feet would shed their coverings and change into talons. I would become generations of eagles, as much a part of the land as any other thing.

But change did not come. I felt only the hot breeze on my face and nothing else.

"Because it is not your true nature," Coyote said. "Think. What is an eagle that you are not?"

Pagán visited the warehouse Lazlo wrote about, pretending to be a new employee. He slipped in through a side door when the others reported for work and hid among boxes and palettes in the storage area. He watched as workers filled orders, walking slowly down rows of high shelves filled with items wrapped for shipping, grabbing a few and placing them in the carts they pushed. When lunchtime arrived, he came out and sat at the end of a long table to listen to their conversations. The workers talked about their pursuits away from the warehouse, trips they might take, hobbies, attending sporting events. They discussed late night television programs and movies they would take their children to see.

Near the end of the break a man in jeans and a white t-shirt sat down across from him. "You're a new guy, huh?" he asked. His forearms were thick with black hair.

Pagán said, "Yes, very new."

"I've been here for twenty three years," the man said.

"Why have you stayed so long?"

The man looked perturbed, as though Pagán's comment had insulted him. "It's a good place to work," he said. "Good people. Think you can fit in?"

Pagán pulled out a paperback copy of Lazlo's book with a large photograph of the author on the back cover, and showed it to the man. "This guy," he said. "Did he ever work here?"

"If he did I never saw him."

"Would you mind asking your coworkers?"

"You a cop?" the man asked. "A P.I.?"

"No, no. Just a fellow writer, trying to find out what kind of a man he was."

The employee took the book and shuffled to a group of people at the center of the table. They passed it around for a minute, each person looking at the photo, some opening the book and reading a sentence or paragraph.

The man came back to Pagán and said, "No one's seen him."

Back in his room that night, Pagán opened Lazlo's fourth

novel, *The Break Room*, about the people in the warehouse. He flipped through the pages, stopping at the beginning of chapter two:

> *Strapping, each of them in their own way, some with muscles and pinched waists, others with curved backs and bowed legs. Appearance doesn't matter, only heart. None of them ever asks for help, their pride is enough to handle the job. Struggle plagues them throughout the year, misfortunes hit like disasters; a hurricane followed by a tornado followed by an earthquake. Sarah needs a math tutor, the roof has a leak and needs to be fixed, the car won't last much longer. But do not tell them how resilient they are; they don't want to hear it. Don't talk about programs and assistance, or the kindness of strangers. Instead, tell them what part of the job is next, that's all they want to know.*

He had enjoyed the book the first time he read it, but now the words sounded pretentious and insincere.

McDormand was drunk, or at least well on the way to drunkenness. "The bastard threatened to kill me," he said. "Accused me of stealing his ideas." He offered Pagán a tumbler of whiskey and Pagán took it. "But then, he could never say I copied that shitty prose of his."

The old man had insisted Pagán call him by his last name, with no title or honorific.

"And he did this at the celebration for your new book," Pagán said.

"It helped his fame to be offensive."

"The media were there?"

McDormand smirked. "*The Times, the Chronicle.* Of course they were there. You don't have a book party without the critics."

"Yes. That was stupid of me."

"I had to reciprocate." McDormand signaled the waiter for

another drink. "I challenged him to a duel. You should have seen the look on him." When the server brought the shot, the writer held it up as if toasting Lazlo. "That would have been fun," he said.

"With guns?" Pagán asked.

"Pistols, at twenty paces. One shot each. A man's game."

"Duels are illegal."

"A writer is an outlaw, by nature," McDormand said. "Have you written anything I've seen?"

"No," Pagán said.

"Maybe someday you will."

"Maybe."

"You already have an in with editors. Who wouldn't want to read the musings of the man who killed Lazlo? And an accident, too. I should have thought of it myself."

Pagán thanked the writer and stood up to leave.

McDormand eyed his drink. "Why don't you stay, my friend? Let me buy you dinner."

Pagán apologized and said he was expected elsewhere.

"It's all right," McDormand said. "Come back tomorrow and we'll do it."

Pagán drove out to the place where the accident had occurred. Bits of their two cars—granules of windshield, plastic from the headlight covers, flakes of chrome—still lay along the shoulder. He found no bloodstains, but in the middle of the road, spattered on the asphalt and the yellow double line, spread a sheen of engine oil and brake fluid, which served in this place as a memorial, as residue of Lazlo's life, and his. There were no tire marks.

For an hour or so he sat in the woods that lined this section of the highway, and watched the traffic as it careened around the curve. Although all the drivers were speeding, none of them crossed the centerlines as Lazlo had. The location of the debris and the oil offered no evidence now of fault. All of it had been dispersed. No one new to the scene could say which driver had flouted the posted signs and painted cautions, or which had encroached on the life of the other.

In the dark hours of the morning, Pagán packed his bag and set it by the door of his room. He sat down to write:

I saw Coyote many times in the weeks that followed. We did not speak, but he watched me from a distance, from hilltops and knolls, and stalked me as I tried to survive in the desert. The days were too hot to forage, and the nights too cold, but hunger and thirst drove me to endure the elements while I searched for the thing I would become. It had been so easy for the others, as though they had known all along where their destinies lay. But each time I thought I had the answer, the land refused me. I pleaded with my former friends for help, to at least provide some clue as to how they had reached the other side, but they could not hear, or chose not to.

In a short time I lost weight, and the heat affected my mind. I wandered among the fauna and the animals with no direction, stumbling into stones, falling, spending hours prostrate on the ground, delirious, begging for a river to bring water and clouds to shade me from the sun. My body receded until my bones stretched my flesh. My mind left itself and I saw the devil at the mouth of a cave, fornicating with a satyr, his exhalations a vile mix of brimstone and venom. Then I knew I would die here, my body fated to become a charred carcass and nothing more. Perhaps Coyote would have his wish after all. He came closer and tracked me from a few paces, awaiting the reward for his patience.

As my strength vanished and I sat waiting for the end, Coyote approached. "You did not find your purpose," he said. "What a waste. You should have taken my advice. None of this suffering was necessary." He pressed his cold nose against my face and licked the salt of my last drops of sweat in anticipation of his feast. He carried the scent of spoiled meat on his breath. His fur boiled with fleas. I turned away from him and looked up at the sky.

It was cloudless, and its empty, pale blue stretched from horizon to horizon, absorbing the prayers and laments of men, as it had done for centuries. Even from the ground I could feel how cold and impassive it was, how impartial and eternal. Because I had spent my time looking down at the land I had never noticed its exquisite beauty.

Coyote bared his teeth and laughed at me. But I lay back and released my spirit to the sky.

Pagán made the bed while the story clattered through the printer. When it finished, he laid a copy in the center of the blanket. He left no other note. Lazlo's books remained in a corner of the room. Perhaps the next occupant would be interested.

His car barely started, and the backfires and howls of the engine may have awakened his sleeping neighbors, or maybe some were still up, having not yet completed their evening's activities. Whatever the case, he apologized, silently, for the disturbance. He pulled out his wallet and counted the money that remained, and tried, in his head, to figure if he had enough to take him to the desert.

Living in Dark Houses

Michael Gale was fifteen when he went down to the basement, took a rifle from the rack and brought it upstairs. He loaded a .30-06 caliber shell, and took careful aim at his father, who rose from the easy chair in which he sat, pointed a drunken finger and ordered him to drop the gun. It was the middle of a humid Long Island summer. Michael Gale betrayed no rage. He said nothing, offered no explanation as he shot his father in the heart. When he saw his father was dead he went out to the front steps, sat on the cool concrete and waited for someone to notice. Two hours later, when the police came, he was still sitting there with the gun beside him and a spot of blood on his finger where he had touched the wound. When the cops asked him if he'd done it he said yes, and when they asked him why he said because it had to be done.

The meticulousness of the act, the cold-bloodedness, despite the fact it appeared unplanned, perplexed the doctors, but as they studied him they learned the abuse to which Michael Gale and his mother had been subjected, the years of beatings and deprivations under the constant threat of worse punishments should they try to leave or seek help.

I knew Michael before the shooting—that is I knew of him—and I knew him after, when he returned to school after two years away. The rumors—the source of almost all information in high school is rumor—said that he'd spent time in a federal prison, occupying a cell with a Mafia hit man who was so impressed by Michael's detachment that he shared his professional secrets and gave him a contact for his capo for when he got out. What then, was he doing back among us, shuffling through Ronkonkoma High's hallways like a specter on his way to social studies?

The other kids avoided him, even the jocks, their bravado about being able to take him notwithstanding, but I felt drawn to him, to that aura of recalcitrance, his lack of regret. At lunch break he didn't eat, but stood outside on the kickball asphalt looking at the sky as though pondering the clouds, or considering other worlds. A teacher always watched him. I'd seen him in the hallways when I was a freshman, but we never spoke. I put my sandwich down and walked past the rows of long tables. Everyone noticed when Michael Gale went by; no one looked up when I did. But I would speak with him.

The bar on the cafeteria door felt cold and resistant, and made a penitentiary sound when I pushed and it recoiled. Outside I saw Michael leaning against the bricks of the gym, with the heel of one foot propped on the wall, hands in the pockets of his jeans, looking very Brando, annoyed but too cool to say so. His hair was short and chopped, almost like he had cut it himself. Autumn blew in unseasonably cold, and the air was the kind of dry that made one's skin hurt. I could feel my lips chapping in the wind, but I didn't lick them because it would look girlish. Best not to get too close. I stopped about ten feet away, so he would know I was talking to him.

"Want this?" I turned my back to Mr. Abernathy and held out a joint I'd rolled in the boys' between periods.

Michael brought his gaze down from the sky and stared, reticent, maybe unsure of what he saw and heard. "Can't do that here," he said at last.

"For later."

He put his hand out. Moving towards him felt like walking on ice, and I began to be nervous about what I looked like and who else besides the teacher might be watching. I dropped the weed into his palm. Michael slipped it into his shirt pocket and said nothing. I watched Abernathy watching us, but as long as we didn't get careless and light up he couldn't see anything. But once the exchange had been made I froze. What should I say now; ask him about the weather? I stared at him and he stared at something in the distance. It wasn't that he wouldn't make eye contact, he just didn't. I wasn't any more important to him than I was to the hordes in the cafeteria. I backed away, and after a minute turned and went inside, but I doubt if he noticed.

After school I waited by the gates. Michael lived on my street and could have taken the bus, but he preferred to walk, and today, so would I. I'd toked halfway down to a roach when he came by. He had no books on him, no supplies, and he wasn't going for the gift I'd laid on him earlier. The other walkers gave him a wide berth like fish around a shark. He moved slowly, and I caught up and then matched his pace.

"Hit?" I said.

He ignored me for a while. At a corner he stopped. "Don't walk with me," he said.

It would have been stupid to ask why, so I didn't, but I shadowed him, giving him another chance to rebuke me, which he didn't take. Instead he walked on as though I wasn't there. Michael moved without destination or purpose, like a zombie forced to roam the earth, or at least as much of it as he could before he finally had to go home for the day. I wondered what waited there for him. The rumors—more rumors—said that his mother never got out of bed anymore, and that a grandmother or aunt had come to run the house. Whoever lived with him was never seen outside, so any of it could have been true. He looked out of place among the other kids, without an overweight bookbag slung over his shoulders, without that hunched posture my classmates joked about of Egyptian slaves pulling another stone for the pyramid of learning. On top of chores and the trouble at home, I had my own studies pressing down on me, inflicting more punishment on my already painful back: a physics book, one for trig, two for English and another for history, all with reading and assignments due within a day or two, which would keep me and everyone else occupied at night, and off these streets, which I guessed was how the parents and administration wanted it.

All that and my father's anger, too, making it so much harder to focus on my studies. Mom begged me to stay with it—keep to the books as my way out. She said if I kept my grades high enough, I could at least get into the community college, where most of the kids I knew would wind up. Stay there and I had a future, she said. I had no choice anyway—if I left, my mother and sister would inherit my share of Dad's wrath.

More years of books and then a job. It didn't seem worth it. Was that the purpose of all this knowledge? I never saw this pyramid we were supposed to be building, only the unimaginative sprawl of our one-story school, surrounded by parking lots and fences, next to a dirt-scarred field that was trod year-round by the football, soccer and lacrosse teams, never left long enough to recover. All that learning supposedly going on, but no monument of knowledge I could see rising from this foundation. The Ronk hadn't changed in the three years I attended. It hadn't changed in thirty years of existence, and I knew it would never change. They'd brought Michael back to prove it.

We went on like that, the two of us walking but not really together, in silence, until we reached our street. I turned to go home, to make sure my mother and sister were okay, get started on a paper, and if Dad allowed it, maybe catch a sitcom later. I stopped, but Michael kept on walking, past our turnoff, into a section of the neighborhood I hadn't ventured into since elementary age. I watched him for a hundred yards or so. He seemed not to diminish as he got farther away, becoming larger somehow, to compensate for the distance. I had to follow.

I tried to see it through his eyes, how he'd raised the rifle against his disbelieving father and lined up the bead on the middle of his chest. His father would be shitfaced probably—some dads always were at that time of day—but would still have the presence to know what was happening and summon the rage we were used to hearing six doors down. It was an anger that took everything personally, from a ball landing on his lawn, to a customer at work changing his mind, to a son's mistakes, and because that was how he saw it, any punishment he decided on fit the crime. I remember that summer echoed particularly loud, and we hadn't seen Michael's mother for a long time. I heard the neighborhood moms whispering she deserved what she got, and had it coming to her for a long time. What she might have done escaped me, but I knew from experience it didn't have to be much. You get on the wrong side of some people and every act becomes an affront, a challenge to what they see as their authority. It could be we were so used to the noise from the Gales' house that on the day of the shooting we didn't think anything unusual happened.

Did his hands shake? Did he hesitate? The newspaper story made it sound like he aimed the gun with the same indifference as if he shot at a tin can. The act of a severely disturbed young man, the police psychologist said. Detached from reality and the consequences of his actions. But just being near Michael I knew that was all bull. I could feel the heat that flooded his brain as he debated the decision to squeeze the trigger, the heat that stayed trapped inside him, no matter how cold he looked to others. He'd have been anything but detached, I knew it, and I sensed he still worked over whether he deserved the purgatory he'd cast himself into, or if, like the experts finally announced, he was not to blame but only reacted on a subconscious, survival level, one that demanded he rescue himself and his mother from the monster that was his father.

Everything we're taught about our parents, from our first smack by the obstetrician, is that they're good and dedicated to caring for us, and that it's a sin to disobey, or not to love them back with all our hearts, because whatever they do is done from love and sacrifice. It takes a lot, an adolescence full of disappointment, before we begin to see it otherwise, to see the egos at play, the selfishness, to feel the hurt of neglect and punishment, before we understand that parents are as capable of hurting as a stranger. Maybe more. And that's when we can accept the responsibility, the stigma of hating a parent. Those thoughts must have confronted Michael as he peered down the barrel of the rifle. He didn't just fire a bullet into his father's heart, he took aim at a whole system, one that gave his father, his abuser, the power of life and death over him, and from which the only way out was to revolt, reverse the violence and seize that power. But by doing so he could never be part of the system again. He usurped and abdicated all at once.

I watched Michael as he walked, and knew he continued to think it over, even though he couldn't now make anything different. He went past rows of houses, every one as lifeless as the school, as though inside the families lived through the same drama as his—the exquisite threat of an icy, angry, regretful father, who saw enemies in every encounter, and who had become a conduit for, instead of a shelter from the cruelty of the world. In a back room huddled the rest of the family, petrified they might set him off. I knew it couldn't be so. There were happy families. I'd seen them. They came out on weekends to play. Their houses lit up in the evenings and looked warm inside. But I hadn't known them the way I knew clans like Michael's. The houses I knew were dark, a stillness punctuated by explosions of temper that echoed through the rooms and hallways. Being in one was like being a front line soldier during a war—violence remained inevitable, unscheduled, unpredictable, and its possibility saturated every minute, every thought.

At the boundary to the town's commercial district Michael stepped into Zeke's Pizza. When I caught up and looked through the window he sat at a table. A waitress delivered a couple of slices, like they'd known he was coming and knew what he wanted before he got there. He looked up at me through the glass as he took his first bite. This time he didn't seem as unfriendly as he'd been on the street. It was more like he was sad about something. I went in and signaled to Zeke for two of my own, and pointed to Michael's table. I went and stood across from him.

"Go ahead," he said.

I pulled out a chair and sat. It felt like a movie. I was sitting down with the don, asking for a favor, wondering what I could do to gain his trust. We'd lived a few houses apart for so long, never talking. Neither one of us played much stickball or touch football in the street with the other kids, or came outside in general, and add in the difference in our ages and the distance became galactic.

"You been following me all the way from school," he said.

"Why do you still go?"

"I have to," he said. "If I don't they put me back in the nuthouse."

"You mean, an asylum?"

"Yeah," he said. "Don't you know I'm a crazy fuck?"

"At least you don't take no shit from the teachers. Man, I wish I could be like that." I felt stupid as soon as I said it. My whole idea had been to be Michael's pal, his equal, almost, but I sounded like a loser kissing up.

"I don't do it to be tough," he said.

I didn't get that. His ignoring the teachers was maybe the coolest thing I'd seen in my days at the Ronk. "Then why?"

"Don't care anymore."

I stared at him. I probably looked like someone's little brother, desperate for attention, but somehow it encouraged him to go on.

"I'm already fucked, so why bother?" he said. "Whatever I do don't make any difference."

"You're not fucked."

"I'm not?" he said. "I killed my old man."

"But he would have killed you, probably."

"And my mother. So what?"

"So you're alive. And she's alive. You had to do it."

Michael ignored my logic and dove into his pizza. This wasn't going where I'd wanted it to. I'd wanted to hang with him, serve as his henchman in whatever scheme or adventure came next. But I realized there was no scheme. Whatever desires and plans Michael had once had been blown away when he pulled that trigger. Maybe if I could get him to talk about it, he'd loosen up. He might dump the guilt out of his system. I looked down at the table. "How bad was it?" I said.

He finished his slices and took a gulp of Coke. Instead of using the napkins he wiped his mouth on his sleeve. "Don't ask me about that," he said.

I stared at him again. It seemed to be my best approach.

"They asked me about it every day for two fucking years." He said it matter of factly, without raising his voice.

"Did he hit you with his hands, or did he use a belt?" I asked. "The sting from leather lasts longer, if you ask me. Probably has something to do with the leverage, the length of the swing. Generates more speed."

Michael narrowed his eyes at me. He sat there for a good thirty seconds, looking at me the way a doctor examines a patient, debating whether to answer. "Everything," he said, finally. "A belt, a baseball bat, the hammer from his work bench. Everything he could think of."

I acted like a different person at home. There were expectations, and we—my mother, sister and I—all tried to live up to them. It created a kind of teamwork among us, each taking a part to get something done, like cooking dinner and cleaning the dishes. This worked completely different from being at school, where everything became a competition. The smart kids competed with each other for the attention of the teachers. The jocks competed with each other for mating rights. Cliques held grudges against other groups, and within them each member fought every other for position in the hierarchy, like chimpanzees. Friendships seemed temporary and conditional. The only constant was the politics. But we had none of that here.

At home there were procedures, and there were, of course, penalties for failure or deviation. My father liked things a certain way, and as long as we adhered we could approximate the happiness of the other families on the block, at least for a few nights out of the week. For example, he did not like to have his thoughts disturbed. If we watched TV while he read the newspaper in his den, and a loud scene came on in the middle of the show, he might hear it. One of my jobs was to anticipate when these scenes might happen—and they do happen in almost every show—and turn down the volume so the interruption became inaudible. I usually kept my hand on the control, just to be safe, so it was easier to prepare myself for the offending segments. But it took something away from our enjoyment of the program. They say you can't miss what you never had, but I did, and still miss the feeling of family. Wanting that life never went away.

Not every disturbance was avoidable. My father had a list he kept tacked up to the side of the kitchen cabinets, which held the names of people who kept him from the success he expected, and believed he deserved. It was neat and official-looking, the names written deliberately, denying the impulse behind it. It included several dozen entries, and next to each a note to remind him of what the person did. Some days, when he added another name, he told us how he would exact revenge, even if it took the rest of his life. Those days it was best not to watch TV at all. I really didn't think he needed the list. He would have remembered all those people and their crimes regardless.

I wondered sometimes why my name, and my mother's and sister's didn't make his list, since it seemed we had offended him more than anyone. Maybe he had another list stashed away just for us. I would have liked to see it, to see if it included our offenses. I'd have liked to know just what, exactly, he had against us.

At home we didn't talk among ourselves about the punishments he doled out, although I think I would have liked to. I'd gotten bigger by high school, and more able to endure them than my sister and mother. But there was nothing I could do to ease their pain. Sometimes, in my room, I heard their whimpers when he became angry. I should have done something, but I didn't. I let them take it because I was still afraid of what he might do to me.

I couldn't help but think Michael and his mother had endured this too. That's the real reason I hounded him. I wanted to know how he got the courage. I wanted to know what would happen to him after the school year ended, and beyond.

The next day I cut the last class and waited for Michael at Zeke's. I paid for his food in advance as an excuse to sit with him again. When he arrived and saw me he stopped at the door. I pointed to the pizza and pushed it closer to his side of the table, and he came over. But when he sat down he said, "Listen, I don't come here to talk. You want to sit here, I don't care. But don't ask me any questions."

We sat for a few minutes, eating, wiping the grease from Zeke's pies off our mouths. Michael squirmed. I had taken the seat that looks out the window, so that he had to sit facing the rear wall, with his back to the door, and it made him uncomfortable, as though he was afraid someone would jump him from behind. I suppose I had taken my seat to avoid the same feeling. But in a minute the silence made me edgy too, the way I felt in the minutes before my father was due home from work. I couldn't just sit there much longer.

"I need your help," I said.

"No, you don't."

"My mother needs your help. My sister."

He looked right at me and I knew he understood. But he said, "Shut up, man. Just shut up about it. What do you think I can do?"

"Tell me how."

He was an inch away from taking a bite, but he put the slice down on the plate, got up and walked out into the darkening afternoon.

There is a private language among the abused. It's not something that can be understood by those who haven't experienced the shame of torture, or how they live with it, or allow it to happen. It describes how we live, as both the cause and the victims. Glances, postures, subtle gestures comprise this language, and what isn't said communicates as much as what is. Because we may not always speak, we learn to say things in other ways. Michael and I did it then. He stopped a few yards outside Zeke's and reached for a smoke. From the way he handled it I knew it was the joint I'd given him. I knew then he would tell me what I was desperate to know.

I sat on a weight bench in the basement of Michael's house. I didn't see anyone home when we entered, so I couldn't put the lie to any of the rumors about how he lived. He'd led me straight downstairs, not stopping to let me see the rooms upstairs, not even turning on the lights. At the bottom of the steps he pulled the strings to a couple of bare bulbs hanging from the joists, creating circles of light like those used for interrogations. Something hissed and I jumped, but it was only a leaky hot water heater. I watched as the trickle from the rusted barrel made its way into a crack in the cement floor. The gun rack still hung on the wall, but sat empty, and probably been since the incident, after the cops confiscated anything dangerous.

I thought he would tell me his version of the story at last, but instead he said, "Take off your shirt." Before I could ask why he had his unbuttoned, and he turned around to show me a scar that ran from his left shoulder halfway down and across his back, a rift in the topography of his flesh. He lifted his arm, and there traced another line, pink and raised, a smaller ridge of mountains. He had the sinewy look of a wrestler, and maybe would have made the squad if he'd avoided the injuries his father inflicted. Still, I could see why the jocks kept their distance.

He moved closer while I dragged my sweatshirt over my head. My shoulder looked moldy in the yellow light, more like a fungus than a bruise. I turned a little to show him my back. The welts from my last beating were fading, but remained painful. He sat down behind me on the bench and touched his fingers to the circular marks that accompanied them, as though reading intricate tattoos. "Sometimes he uses a cigarette," I said.

I thought he only wanted to see the evidence, to make sure my story and my motives were true, but while he sat behind me, Michael rested his head between my shoulder blades, and I felt the soft stubble of his beard against a still sore area of skin. I let him keep it there. The pressure didn't hurt, and I began to think he had some power to cure me.

"Why is there no one else home?" I asked.

"There's no one else to be home."

"Your mother?"

He lifted his head from my back. "She left after I came home and the semester started. I don't even know where she went."

"She wouldn't forgive you?"

"Would you?"

It didn't make sense. "He beat her as much as he did you," I said.

"More. He put her in the hospital. She was only back for a few days when he went after her again."

"And that's when you did it."

Michael remained quiet, and I didn't push for an answer. The details didn't really matter at this point. He moved away to the other side of the basement, as if waiting for me to follow him back upstairs. He shed no tears, displayed no anguish over the departure of his mother. He did not seem, even, to be trying to figure this aspect of his tragedy out, but had accepted the fact she'd left. I wanted to tell him to call the police, have them track her down for child abandonment, but I realized then his abandonment occurred long before. I might have insisted he come to my house. He could have dinner with my family, watch a little TV, stay in the spare bedroom overnight, or for a few days if he wanted. But of course that wasn't possible either.

"Do you want me to stay here?" I asked. "We could hang out, maybe talk. You wouldn't have to be here by yourself."

"What is there to talk about?" he said.

"Then we don't have to talk."

A clock chimed upstairs. I didn't have to count the bells to know it was five and getting dark, and that I hadn't begun clearing the yard of leaves. It had to be done before he got home. "If I see a leaf on that lawn it's your ass," he'd said.

"Mom," I said aloud. I had to tell her to take Susan and get out of there. I had to run home and bring them to Michael's house where we could all be safe. But he would come. Or he would stop them before they could leave. I had to get back, right away. I wouldn't make them take my punishment.

"I know you have to go, Tim," Michael said as I gathered my bag. He understood what was going down. His look said he would have done the same thing.

"Wait for me at Zeke's tomorrow," I said. I bolted up the stairs and ran the six-house distance, flinging my gear into the garage and grabbing the rake. I attacked those leaves as though they were alive, like they were an army advancing on my mother and sister. But a breeze blew in—a gentle thing that for someone else might invoke calm or beauty. I tried my best, but it did no good. Leaves littered the yard and kept coming in from the neighbor's. I worked until it became so dark I couldn't see, and laid the last bag at the side of the garage. He watched me finish and came at me as soon as I was done.

The gun was easy enough to obtain. The discontent at our school ran deep, and someone would always flout the law for profit, or sometimes just for fun. That made weapons and drugs common knowledge, available with the right contact and the proper amount of cash. Even the nerds could get a gun, if they ever wanted to. I stashed it in my backpack, inconspicuous among the books, just another lump of learning breaking my back.

"One shot," I told Michael. "Just like you."

"And what good will it do?" he asked. "They'll hate you. You think they'll thank you for it, but they won't. You'll be like me."

Neither one of us ate today. The four slices of pizza sat on the plates, as frigid as the weather outside.

"That was my mistake," he said. "Thinking that she cared."

"He's alone at the house," I said. "My mother and Susan went out grocery shopping. I'm going to do it." I started to get up from the booth.

"You really want to fuck up your life that much?"

"It's like you said, Michael. I'm already fucked. I guess the question is what kind of fucked do I want to be?"

"Just get away," he said. "Steal the car and drive someplace and stay there. Not this."

"I'm not doing this just for me," I said.

"Sure. That's what I thought."

So they would put me away for a while. But no one could touch me wherever it was, and Mom and Susan would be safe, even if they didn't thank me—even if they said they hated me. I could live with that more than the idea of them being hurt. And I would get used to being alone. I would be better at it than Michael. I would prefer it.

He had shown me, in his way, what I needed to know. I paid the tab over his protest, and slipped my backpack onto my shoulder, which caused me to wince a little from my last beating. I felt glad for the pain, for the encouragement it offered.

"I don't know if I'll see you again," I said, which was true but far too dramatic, and I regretted it. This didn't play like the end of a movie, where the two buddies embrace each other, knowing that one of them isn't going to make it. In this scene, we didn't even shake hands.

The cold air slapped my face when I opened Zeke's door and stepped outside. This would be one of those unrelenting winters, where the snow and the ice start right around Thanksgiving and keep the world frozen until April. I thought about who might shovel the driveway in the coming months, and how much worse the weather would be upstate if it was going to be that bad here. I passed the houses of the neighborhood, unconcerned the families would know a gun rested in my pack, even wanting to stop and tell them about it. I wanted to say, "I'm doing this for you, too."

My father would motivate me, I had assumed, but all that simply drained away as I walked. Everything became calm. I carried a certain amount of pride, too—that I'd finally come to a point where I could act, that I could make things right, and that the consequences were not important. No heat tortured my mind, like it had Michael's. The debate had ended, and I knew it wouldn't haunt me in the future the way it did him.

When I got to my house I slipped around to the side door and into the garage. I started to close the door behind me, but something blocked it. Michael pushed it open—so hard that it threw me back and I let go of the backpack. He came in and picked it up before I could, undid the zipper and pulled out the gun.

"How?" I said. I hadn't seen him following me.

He scrutinized the pistol as though it were a toy, perhaps not up to the job. He flipped open the cylinder to inspect the rounds. I'd lied. I hadn't been sure if I could do the job with one shot, like Michael, and I'd loaded all six chambers. He took out four of the bullets and threw them to the garage floor. "This is all that's needed," he said. Then he snapped the cylinder shut and spun it. He pointed it at me.

"Michael, you have to let me," I said. "I have to end this."

"It is ended," he said.

He moved to the door that led into the house and jiggled the knob. "Open it," he said.

I unlocked it, and he took my key. As he stepped inside he asked me where he would find my father, and I told him. Then he closed the door and locked it again. I heard him pad down the hallway to the living room, where my father was surely sitting, reading the paper and swilling a beer. Michael's footsteps diminished and I listened harder, anticipating father's raised voice, the rage and indignation, and dreading the eternity between the first shot and the second.

The Sting of the Glove

    Luis sleepwalked back to our corner, like he was having a bad dream. Maybe we all were. Grillo charged through the ropes and I ducked in after him. He got hold of Luis's arm and led him to the stool. The kid had taken a step towards the wrong corner after the bell, and the ref had to turn him around. He crash-landed into the seat, sucking air like his oxygen had run out in the middle of the last round. It was so motherfuckingly hot in the arena I could barely breathe myself. Luis looked bad—he was a slick mass of flesh slumped back against the corner cushions, more like an accident victim than a boxer. His face was raw from the beating he was taking and his black hair was drenched into little spikes from sweat. His muscle tone was going. He was loose and pallid. That's the sign that a man is losing control of his body, that it won't respond to his commands. It means trouble. But there were only two rounds to go. I was sure he could make it through. I'd trained him hard to get to this fight, this moment. He just had to will it. More fights are won on guts than talent. But then, what I heard I couldn't believe: Luis said he'd had enough. He said he couldn't go out for the ninth and that I should tell the ref to call it.

"It's just two more rounds," I said. I couldn't hear myself talk. The crowd noise made it tough enough, but it was the air, so soaked with humidity that it knocked the words down before they could travel. Luis stared past me, a zombie, and I slapped him to get his attention. "Two more rounds, Luis! Six minutes and you fight for the title."

"I don't care," he said between gasps. "I can't stand up no more. Can't do it."

Grillo was all over the kid's face—a swab up the nose, the compress on his cheekbone. The worst was the cut under the right eye. Cardenas opened that in the fourth and we hadn't been able to get it to stop bleeding. It was puffed out to where his eye was half closed, so he couldn't see the left hooks coming. Grillo slopped a palm full of Vaseline over it and I heard Luis grunt from the pressure.

"You can't quit. It's a title shot, dammit," I said. "You won't get another."

He just kept saying, "No, no, no. Too tired."

"But you're ahead." I told him this even though I knew it wasn't true. "Just dance with him for two rounds and you'll win on points." Usually I tell a fighter the opposite. If he's ahead I say he's losing, so he won't ease up. It seemed crazy to lie like this, but what choice was there? I never had a quitter before, and I wouldn't let him be my first.

When Luis first heard of the possibility of this fight he said he would take it for free just to have a shot at a belt. He wanted it, and I wanted him to have it. Now that he'd come so close I wouldn't let anything stand in his way—not even his own limits.

I looked to the side and there was Marisa in the first row. She was standing on her toes, screaming something I couldn't hear, her arms flailing like a crazy person. She was a skinny muchacha—all lip gloss and fingernails, and a half dozen bracelets jangling on her forearms. Skimpy tops and tight jeans all the time, like sex on parade. Always jumping and yelling instructions—take him out, Luis! The left! The left! Standing on her seat until the people behind begged her to sit down. I don't know how many seconds I blew staring.

I moved a little so I couldn't see her.

"I'm not stopping the fight," I told Luis.

And he said, "Please." Like a baby.

That pushed me too far. "Then go in there and tell the ref yourself. You go in and say, 'Excuse me sir, but I give up. I'm a quitter, and I want everyone to know it.'" I was screaming at him. I was dripping sweat and having my own trouble breathing. Goddam humidity. "Now get back in there and win this thing."

Grillo looked at me as he worked over the kid's face. He was a mess too, panting like a dog just from his work between rounds. But we had no choice on the location—Cardenas wanted it in front of his homies and he had the higher ranking, so we were stuck in Modesto. Go outside and you could have smelled the cow shit.

The crowd wanted him back out there too. They wanted to see him go down, to take one of the home boy's big left hooks to the skull and watch the blood and sweat fly off Luis's head as it snapped back like a broken doll's. I know how they are. The bloodier it gets, the louder they get. They don't give a damn about the sport or the science—they just want to see someone get killed.

I stuffed the water bottle into Luis's mouth, but he spit it out. "Drink!" I yelled.

The ring girl caught the big number nine on the ropes and almost dropped it as she stepped out. The men in the crowd whistled when she bent over. Then the tone for seconds out. "Help him up," I said to Grillo.

Luis used the ropes to brace his arms. Grillo kept slopping grease on his face from behind until the ref ordered him to stop. I told Luis to keep the gloves up and protect his face, but I knew he couldn't hear me. Our corner man grabbed the stool away, then held the ropes wide for me. I took a step through and looked again at Marisa. His hip-hop honey, he calls her. She was jumping up and down on stiletto heels. Her hair was flying like it was underwater. And the world's tightest leather pants.

Grillo nudged my shoulder and said, "Es no bueno."

I thought he'd caught me looking at her, but then I saw he was still looking at Luis as he staggered into the ring. "No mas," Grillo said. "No mas. ¿Por qué haces esto?"

I didn't answer. I was staring down the judges. Of course, they were avoiding me. There they were, ringside in their nice suits, trying to look respectable, three stiffs who probably knew less about boxing than any three dumbshits in the audience. If Luis made it through, they would decide his future. Unless someone had paid them in advance and it was already decided, that is.

The bell. The ref made Cardenas wait while he checked Luis out. He called to me, "You sure he's okay?" The ref was a sub. They brought him in at the last minute. Who knew if he'd ever worked a big fight before?

I told him Luis was fine.

Cardenas was waiting, tapping his gloves together. He was a bull pawing at the ground, waiting to charge. When the ref signaled them to box he ran across the ring and laid into Luis with two jabs and an uppercut. Luis leaned back against the ropes, tried to keep his hands up, but Cardenas swatted them away like the mosquitoes in that dump and wailed on him with two of those legendary hooks. I could hear the impacts even above the ecstasy of the crowd. Luis was still standing, somehow. Cardenas turned to the ref as if to ask why he didn't stop the fight. I was wrong. Why didn't I see it? The heat must have fogged my brain. I felt Grillo brush past me with the towel, and he took a step up to the apron, but it didn't matter. Luis fell like the South Tower, rubble on the canvas.

The ref didn't even bother to count.

I followed Grillo into the ring and had to push through a wall of bodies just to get to Luis. Cardenas's people, our people, security people, media people—every one of those dickheads jumped in as soon as the fight was over, like they were going to get their face on cable or something. The doctor was working to revive Luis. Marisa was bouncing behind a row of rent-a-thugs, trying to get closer, to see the damage to her husband.

Boxing doesn't get news coverage unless it's something bad like corruption. So naturally, when Luis went into a coma I started getting calls from newspapers and a couple of ring rags, and one from the state boxing goons that kept me on the line for an hour. Some jerkoff who kept asking me for the specific details—that's how he kept saying it, "I want specific details, Mr. Sharkey"—especially what I said to Luis before that last round.

It was three days after the fight and I was beat from dealing with the pressure. I went to Luis's hospital room. Felt real bad about what happened. And they say people in comas can hear your voice too, so I thought I could give him a few minutes of encouragement before I had to get back to the gym.

As I got near the door I heard Marisa's voice. She wasn't there the day before when I stopped by, which struck me as strange. Hearing her made me nervous about going in. What if she blamed me for his injuries? What if, like those media saps seem to think, she believed I pushed him too hard, that his condition was my fault?

But before I could leave, Marisa came out of the room and practically ran into me. Her bracelets made like a wind chime when she stopped short. She was wearing tight jeans and four-inch heels again. Her halter top was like a second skin. At first I thought how wrong it was for her to be wearing that at a time like this. She might arouse the docs as well as me. But what was she supposed to wear? It wasn't like she was in mourning.

"Hey Eddy," she said. "Thank God."

"You're leaving?"

"If I don't get away from those lunatics I'm going to kill one of them." She took my elbow and started leading me down the hallway. She was talking, but I all I could concentrate on was the way her hand felt against my arm. It was like a teenager's hand, all soft and delicate. And I know that sounds perverse, but that's what it felt like.

"Gonna kill who?" I said.

"His mother and sister." She started waving her hands. "They think I should sit here all day with him, like a good little girl. Hey, I got a life to live too. I don't want to sit here all afternoon and listen to that old woman's voodoo."

Her voice was light and a little raspy. It was a sex kitten voice, even though she wasn't trying to be sexy. I thought maybe she'd been crying, too. "What's their problem?" I asked.

"They think they're still in El Salvador, that's their problem. His mother calls me names in Spanish and makes his sister translate it, and I know she ain't telling me everything the bitch said. I think she's putting some kind of spell on me."

"All this time I thought you spoke Spanish."

"Uh uh. The only way I know Luis is cursing at me is from the tone of his voice."

So she was no muchacha. I never would have guessed. Whenever I saw her with Luis I just assumed. "He curses at you?"

"I guess it runs in the family."

I looked at her closely. I didn't see any bruises, just skin—smooth, nut colored, not a freckle or a blemish, and all I could think of was running my tongue from her bare shoulders down the middle of her back. I had to shake my head before the fantasy got worse. I thought about Luis's temper. "Does he hit you?"

She looked back, right into my face. Maybe she was taking in the bend in my nose or the little scar on my cheek. Maybe she was checking the gray in my hair. I should have turned away, but I didn't, and looked right back at her. She ignored my question. Instead she said, "You have really nice eyes. They're so blue."

I said, "I guess I do." That was stupid. Sometimes what I think and what I say get mixed up, like I have a wire loose up there, like maybe a punch from one of my fights gave me a short circuit.

I should mention how lucky I am the eyes made it through six years in the ring without getting mashed like the rest of me. But I kept that quiet. I wanted to compliment Marisa back, but then she might have thought I was hitting on her. Her husband was in there, for chrissake—my boxer, in a coma, with his mother sitting next to him. Who knew what Marisa would think?

"Let me go in there and talk to them. Maybe I can calm them down."

"Good luck with that," she said, and she shook her bracelets through her hair. I don't know why, but I wanted to hold her tight right then. To put my hands around her twig of a waist and pull her in. It was so stupid—I'm maybe twice her age and I know we have nothing in common except maybe a love of the ring.

Once the mother and sister found out who I was, they started with the insults. The mother gave it to me in Spanish—I heard bastardo and gringo and even puto. From a woman who doesn't even come up to my armpit. The sister came at me in English, pointed a finger in my face and said I should watch out for myself. Normally, I'd give it right back to them, but for the moment I was happy that I could deflect some of the anger they had for Marisa towards me, and I just took it. I tried to get closer to Luis, to look into his face, but the mother jumped up and stood in my way. She put her hands on her hips and kept on bad-mouthing me. I wanted to swat the attitude right off her face. The sister said, "Why don't you just go now?" It was a good idea, so I did, and when I got out into the hallway, Marisa was gone.

*

She was with him the first time Luis came into the gym and said he wanted to box. I'd heard about him from some of the boys I was training. They said he was good, but that he hated his manager. They said they'd send him my way if I wanted.

They looked like a couple of high school kids on a first date—skank city, both of them. She had on this old tube top and a pair of jeans full of holes. Skinny as she was, there was enough skin showing to make me look twice. In her heels she was taller than him. He was still featherweight at the time, same weight as me when I started fighting. Had his pants pulled down practically to his knees, with about four inches of underwear showing. First thing I said to him was if he wanted to work out with me he'd have to pull those chinos up and dress right from now on.

I could tell he didn't like that, so I pushed harder. I asked to see his ID to make sure he didn't need parental permission. He got mad and made a big show about them being married, as if that made a difference to me. I just nodded. I took him over to the medicine ball and said it would be a while before he could put the gloves on. I thought he was going to quit right there, but Marisa came over and said he'd better do what I said, because I was the one with experience.

If she only knew. I'd been running the gym for a few months and was in way over my head. The bills were huge. I was willing to sign up just about anyone with two hands. If Marisa had said she wanted to box, I would have laced her up too. As for my teaching experience, all I knew was what my old trainer did to me. I hadn't put any of the guys in the ring yet. The whole operation was on a shoestring—a frayed shoestring at that. But I had to look tough to them. They expected it.

There's a room in the bowels of the gym where I retreat sometimes. It has no windows and stinks of cigarettes, but it's a good place to think. I don't get interrupted there. Sometimes I use it to make decisions about fights and fighters—like who's earned a bout for the open middleweight spot on Saturday's undercard at the arena. I thought I would give that one to Bobby Smits. He's been showing improvement lately.

Sometimes I hide in there and watch film. I like to watch the big fights. The classics. Ali-Frazier, Tyson-Douglas, Hagler-Hearns, Duran-Sugar Ray. If I'm lucky I get the recordings without the dumbass announcers. Then it's just me and the two fighters, and I turn up the sound so I can feel every punch vibrate like I was connected to those two guys, like when I was fighting. The building, the media, the crowd—they vanish—and the whole universe becomes that one guy across from you. For an hour or so he is all that stands between you and everything you dream about—respect and money and fame—and he wants to steal it from you. You know he'll do whatever he has to. He'll hold and kidney punch and head butt—just like you will. You get to know the feel of him leaning on you, the smell of his sweat in your face, the sting of his gloves. In just a few seconds you learn to hate every piece of him.

Maybe that was what was wrong with Luis—he didn't hate Cardenas enough to beat him. I was in that room, in the dark, watching a video of the fight for the third time. The spectre of his body flashed in a clockwise circle, jabbing and ducking to keep away from Cardenas's power, like I told him to do. For a while it worked. Cardenas got frustrated that Luis wouldn't let him get close and left himself open to counterpunches. But by the fourth it all changed. Luis got caught in a corner. Cardenas shouldered him and threw an uppercut. Instead of holding, Luis tried to trade shots, like a street fight, and Cardenas got in the heavier blows. I was screaming at him to clinch, but he wouldn't listen. Stupid kid.

It was really over right there. I started looking for clues that he couldn't go on, that I should have stopped the bout sooner. They seemed everywhere—his hands were lowered, the bounce was gone from his steps. Between rounds I leaned closer to the screen to look at his face, to see if I could determine when he lost his awareness and began fighting on instinct alone. But instead I watched myself as I climbed into the ring and knelt in front of Luis. How I turned to look, just for a second, towards Marisa as I pulled through the ropes. And again while I was barking instructions, and once more as I went back to the apron. My face went blank each time I took her in. Watching the DVD it was like I was spying on a stranger. Everything I saw I condemned.

When the replay was over I turned on the lights and took the letter out of my pocket. The state commission is conducting a formal investigation into the fight, and they set a day and time for me to be interrogated. It's a face-saver with Luis in a coma, something they do whenever a boxer gets hurt to wash their hands of any potential blame. Something to convince themselves and the public that a sport where two guys get paid to beat each others' brains in isn't too dangerous. Jesus H. Christ, who do they think they're kidding?

If they think it'll help with publicity, they'll discipline me and suspend the ref to make themselves look good. What's a couple of low-lifes compared with the boys in the suits? Even if I'm cleared, I wouldn't be surprised if the mother slaps a lawsuit on me out of spite.

The next day I called Marisa to find out if there was any news about Luis, because I didn't want to face the El Salvadoran Mafia again. Took me a few minutes to work up the nerve—we never really talked much before. She said she didn't go see him either. "I can't deal with them," she said. She did call the doc, though, and he said no change. The usual: "All we can do is wait and hope."

Then I asked Marisa if she wanted to go somewhere and get a drink.

*

After two years training with me the kid had won all six of his bouts, and his fights actually made us some money. My training program consisted of me trying not to fuck up his style too much. I'm only kind of kidding there—I could see he had potential. A couple of promoters told us he reminded them of a young me. I didn't think so. I told Luis he was gonna be much better. I didn't want to move him too fast, but of course he wanted to box every week. I brought in Grillo, who was a big help. He made him train right, no sloughing off, and it worked. Luis was tougher and learning some ring smarts. And having Luis do so well was like TV ads for the gym. The local kids lined up for a spot on my training schedule.

Marisa came in almost every day after her work to watch and cheerlead. She always had on something tight, which was great because it made the other guys train harder to show off for her. Well, most of them. I noticed one of my guys, Xerxes—man, where do they get these names—took a lot of time out from his workout to hang around her. He was a heavyweight, about two thirty-five. Chiseled like a Greek statue, so I guess the name fits. Black like night and hard like a diamond. With a shaved head so he looked like he was from the future. But with a body like that he figured he didn't have to train hard. Grillo and me were always after him to get serious.

I saw them talking a few times over in a corner, while Luis was sparring, away from where he could see. I went over to tell Xerxes to get back to the speed bag, and I heard them feeling each other up with words. He said, "What you doin' with that burrito boy? You can do better than that."

"You mean like you?" she said.

"Maybe. If you feel lucky."

"You better watch your mouth. Luis go crazy on your ass, he sees you talking to me."

"Him? Be like a fly. Like a mosquito." Then he made a buzzing noise and slapped his palms together hard. You could hear the smack across the floor. He rubbed his hands together and pretended to let something fall away. "That your boy down there," he said.

"You're really something," she said. "Talking like that to a married lady."

"I don't see you running away," he said.

The next couple of weeks I noticed Marisa didn't show up every day like usual, and neither did Xerxes. I didn't have to guess what was going on. Luis, though, he told me she was with her mother, or a friend. The kid just wanted to box. If he wasn't concerned, neither was I.

Six months later, still no losses and Luis is ranked. Sounds a lot better than it is—that just shows you how screwed up this business is—one or two good fights and you can get ranked. Offers for decent bouts came in all the time. Me and Grillo tried to pick the ones where Luis had the best chance of winning and staying on the ladder.

Then Cardenas's people called. He was the number one welterweight. They said they wanted to give Luis a break—and me and Grillo too. Right away I suspected they were looking for a tune-up fight—a punching bag for Cardenas before he goes in against the champ. I wanted to tell them to go fuck themselves, but I didn't. Thirty-five Gs plus fifteen percent of the gate. That was a good start and I even talked them up a little more. But still I wasn't sure, so I got Grillo in to go over the options, to ask him if Luis was ready for this kind of competition.

We were in my office talking. Grillo, Mr. Negative, said Luis needed at least six more months and two fights before he'd be ready. I said maybe not, maybe he could handle Cardenas, but then, I could have been seeing dollar signs. And of course who walked in on the conversation—both of them this time. Once they got the details they were all over me to call back and take the deal. Marisa pushed it even harder than Luis. I could see her imagining all the junk she was going to buy with the payday.

So it was Luis's big chance. But I knew it was risky. Cardenas was stronger, more experienced. Luis gets beat bad, we might lose the ranking and be right back where we started. But for fuck's sake, I'm the kid's manager. I had to believe in him. So I pushed him. Harder than he was ever pushed. Roadwork, just like the old days. All day on the bags and in the ring. It was weird, but the harder I trained him, the more he seemed to appreciate it. I told Napo, his sparring partner, to make him work, to fight back—never let the kid think it's going to be easy. Then, when he couldn't stand up anymore, we watched tape of Cardenas. Every fight in the last two years, over and over. I wanted Luis to know every move he might throw—to obsess about this guy. I wanted him to be screwing Marisa at night and see Cardenas under him instead. It was the only way he would be ready.

First thing Marisa asked me when we met is what my record was as a fighter. I was always proud that I won more than I lost. It's just a little thing that keeps me going.

She had on this little tank top, and even in the bad light of the bar I could see she wasn't wearing a bra. I couldn't help thinking that was for me. She ordered another lemon drop martini, which pissed off the waitress because the bartender didn't make the first one the way Marisa likes them and she made her take it back. But I gave the waitress a look that said, "just do your job, honey," and she took off. I thought Marisa liked that.

"So Eddy," she said, "did you ever fight for a title?" Man, her voice just goes right into the heart of me.

"Victor Robinson," I said. "A piece of the middleweight belt." I started remembering it—we slugged on each other for twelve.

"And I had him beat."

"So you won."

"I beat him," I said, "but I didn't win. Split decision. You ask me, I think somebody got to the judges." Sometimes I think everything associated with this game is crooked.

Before she could ask if I got a rematch I told her Robinson's people wouldn't go for it. "That's another way I know I won. They knew he couldn't beat me so they wouldn't let him fight me again."

It felt good to talk about those days with Marisa. Like she understood. Ever since Barbara left me I missed that. It's one thing to shoot the shit with Grillo and the guys, but having a woman who can talk boxing—who's willing at least to rub your shoulders and let you bitch about the bad deals and the bad luck and the injuries—and then tell you it's all right because you're giving it everything and nobody could ask for more. That's pretty rare. Thinking about it, I never really had it that great with my ex, either. We were both on the rebound, so courtship was a couple of nights in Vegas, and the honeymoon was the next two. When we sobered up we both knew it was over, but for some reason she thought I had bucks and made the divorce a nightmare. Took me six months to get out of it. She took my house and took all the fight out of me along with it. So I hung up the gloves. But I always thought I had a few more bouts left in me.

Being stupid again, I asked Marisa how she and Luis got together. I didn't mean to bring him up. Was I punch drunk or what?

"I always had a thing for guys who could fight," she said. "When I was with Luis, I felt safe, like he could protect me no matter what. I liked how strong his hands were." She dipped her finger into her drink and started drawing circles on the tabletop. "Now, though …"

"Now … what?"

"I never thought I'd see him like this," she said. "What's he gonna be like when he recovers?" She flipped her hand and the bracelets jabbered. "If he recovers. What if he stays like that?"

I pictured them, in the hospital room. Luis and his mother and sister, like a photograph in the paper of some tragedy in Central America that we're supposed to feel sorry for—those poor people, how do they live like that? How do they take it? And then turn the page and go back to our daily business.

I wanted to tell Marisa not to worry, that he'd get better. But, no. I wanted to tell her he'd never wake up and that she should get on with her life. All I could say is, "You deserve better. You shouldn't have to deal with all this shit."

She looked me in the eyes again and said, "You're great, Eddy."

I felt like I was back in the arena in Modesto. My head was in the heat again. Whatever I did or said, it was going to be the wrong thing. She kept on talking, telling me about all the things she wanted to do in her life, all the things that Luis had said they'd have to wait for because he still had to support his mother and sister. She was talking like I was the first person to listen for a long time. I could tell how rough it had been on her. I didn't even have to ask. That mother-in-law and sister giving her grief, and Luis hasn't been no prince either. I waved the waitress over for another round.

I walked her to her car. I took her hand. I saw how gnarled up mine was compared to hers, which was all smooth and tiny and neat. I leaned over and give her a little kiss, on the corner of the mouth. She put her other hand on my shoulder and kissed me back. She got in the car and I watched her drive away. Why the fuck did she kiss me back?

Two days later I sat in the hospital lobby behind a newspaper until the mother and the sister went out for lunch, then went up to Luis's room. He was yellow and puffy. His face still had contusions from the beating he took. His stomach went up and down with the clicks of the respirator. "I didn't mean for this to happen," I said. "Any of it." I couldn't think of anything else to say, and I stared at him for a couple of minutes, remembering some of the fights he won. There was one against that Collins kid—Luis was a big underdog but he knocked him out in seven. When the ref counted to ten Luis ran across the ring and jumped into my arms, like a son coming home from the war. He was so emotional he told me he loved me.

I didn't want to think about what his life would be like when he came out of the coma—if he came out. That was too painful. Everything now is too painful.

Saturday night, I'm sitting on the steel table taking deep breaths. Grillo is behind, arms around me, fingers locked, pulling up on my ribs, muttering "loco" and "es stupido." "¿Por qué?" he keeps saying. "¿Por qué?"

Why? I don't have an answer he'd understand. I try to visualize the opponent, but all I see are the four walls of green blocks around us. I think of how I need to apologize to Smits later for pulling him from the card at the last minute.

Grillo tells me I need to work up a sweat, to loosen up, but I don't want to spend energy I might need later. I still work out with the boys, but I don't spar. It's nothing like fighting shape. I'll be going on guts and experience.

It's only six rounds, I tell myself. Grillo pulls at my hand like he's mad at me, tells me to hold it still while he shoves the glove onto my right. The fit is a little off, but I don't complain. I curl my fingers and push against the lining.

I wonder if Marisa got the ticket I left for her. If I'll be able to see her when I peek over my opponent's shoulder, when I fall to the seat in between rounds.

Nixon in State

After an hour we had moved maybe fifty feet, and I felt responsible for the disappointment on Mina's face, in the same way I'd taken the blame for our breakup last year. All my fault because I couldn't commit. The line of mourners stretched to an intersection as far away as the horizon. People in front of us said the wait was ten hours or more, which meant we wouldn't view the body until well after midnight, maybe not until morning. I would miss work the next day gladly, but I had no idea how long Mina and the Van Burens would be willing to hang.

We'd come up on a whim—nothing better to do on a Monday evening, and we were all involved politically, although sometimes on opposite sides, and how long could it take to get a glimpse of the disgraced president, the only man ever to quit the highest office in the land? We wanted to see him before his infamy passed completely from the public consciousness, to see if he looked as crooked in death as he did in front of the cameras.

But at the pace we were moving it might never happen. Carol and Phil looked okay—they held hands like two kids on a date—

but Mina stood with her arms crossed, shifting from one foot to the other and staring down the road as if planning an escape. She wanted history and a night worth remembering. Instead she got Carol going off like a radical journalist.

"Maybe we should have brought lawn chairs and a barbecue grill," I said. "Make it a tailgate party." I smiled in case they thought I was serious.

I wanted to keep the women from arguing. The war of words had started almost as soon as we joined the queue. "I'll believe he's dead when I see him lying in front of me." Carol hated Nixon. Every statement, every decision he made when he served as president provoked her liberal's wrath, even before Watergate. His death, two decades after his term, induced in her the kind of unabashed glee usually reserved for the demise of war criminals or mass murderers.

Which didn't sit well with Mina. She was DAR, like her mother, and despised the left as much as Tricky Dick. "What about the good he did? What about China, and the Soviets? He made us safe."

"Safe from what? The yellow horde going to roll up on the beach in San Francisco Bay next week?" Carol animated her logic with sweeps of her hands, and a Hopi necklace that rattled each time she gestured.

I pulled Mina away before the two of them could get into it further. "It's really good to see you," I said, repeating myself from two hours ago. "How's married life?"

A stupid question, but I was anxious to defuse them. And curious as well. The marriage was a rebound affair, I was sure. She and what's-his-name got hitched four months after we called our relationship off. We hadn't seen each other since then. Why I'd even phoned her today continued to sit in some dark, personal courtroom of my consciousness, waiting to be judged. "Nixon's lying in state in Yorba Linda," I'd said. "The Van Burens and me are going up to view the body. How often do you get to see a dead president?" I guess I thought I owed it to her. And I didn't want to be the Van Burens' third wheel.

She said yes so fast I didn't have a chance to invite her husband, and then I wouldn't.

But this time her response sounded measured, as if she searched for the right words, the proper public statement. "Rob and I are very happy," she said. No elaboration. No dreamy reverie as she remembered nights of hours-long lovemaking, or recounted their dozens of shared interests and friends. She didn't smile, either. More like annoyance at being asked, like I should know it wasn't possible for any newlywed not to be happy. But then, since I was the one who destroyed our relationship, how could I know? Her curt answer reminded me of how unmarriageable I remained.

"You know…" Carol started round two. "I think when I get there, I'll stare at him for eighteen minutes." Her husband laughed at the reference to the gap in Nixon's tapes, but he muffled it with a hand over his mouth, and searched the line in both directions to see if she'd offended anyone. The Van B's flaunted their eccentricities—she in her peasant dress and he in shoulder-length hair and a Sex Pistols t-shirt. When they dressed like hippies during Nixon's term they helped put faces on the counterculture movement, but by 1994 they were late thirties and tragically unhip.

Me? I never liked Nixon that much. Seriously, who did? He had no friends in Congress and certainly none in the press, but because he was a president, and a Californian, and because he fuck you'd the Washington establishment by decreeing his body not lie in state at the Rotunda, as custom dictated, I would gladly go along for a respectful last look.

That is, until we saw the line. We drove for twenty minutes to find the end; wound up parked in some residential neighborhood that we'd have to take a taxi back to once we got to the viewing, if we could even remember where it was. All these people…the scale of the queue made accurate estimates, at least from my perspective, almost impossible. Ten thousand? Twenty thousand? Many sounded boisterous—a festival mood—a conga line instead of the somber procession the situation called for. We opened the windows while we cruised and listened to people recap sound bites from Nixon's career like sports highlights: the secret bombing of Cambodia, the debates with Kennedy, the desperate vindictiveness of his Checkers speech.

"Are you sure?" I kept asking as we looked for a space. "Sure you want to do this?"

Phil said, "Oh, yeah. We've been waiting twenty years." I had directed my question to them, but intended it for Mina. She stared out the Subaru's window at the crowd. I'd hoped her seeing such a turnout for the man would cheer her, but maybe she had something else on her mind. Probably that she should have insisted Rob come too. Sure, I would have been thrilled to be jammed against his hip while he made out with his wife, my ex.

I assessed the happy faces and imagined they didn't come to honor a statesman as much as to stand close to a dead celebrity, to experience the entertainment value it promised. To them it was a media event. They would have come out if it had been Sinatra or Bob Dylan or even one of the Monkees lying there.

Carol kept up her rant, and made sure the people around us could hear. "This is so great," she said. "All these people coming out to have the last laugh on that clown. He screwed this country so bad…"

But she'd misread the crowd—at least the part of it who'd supported Nixon, whatever he did. Phil cringed as heads turned to see the source.

Every few minutes we moved five or ten feet. We sat in the traffic jam leading to an accident, cursing the lucky ones at the scene for gawking and making us wait longer than necessary, yet knowing we'd loiter too, once we got there. The residents of the nearby houses peeked, occasionally, from behind their curtains, guarding their tidy yards, checking to see if the line had finally moved past their property. Instead it kept getting longer, and I could sense the worry coming from inside those bungalows that people would begin to trespass and vandalize. We were so far from the viewing that patriotism and respect would be on hold for a while.

"If you're not here to honor the President, why are you here?" A baritone with a tinge of the South. Someone who had overheard Carol—a porcine man in shorts and an Angels ballcap, clutching a little American flag that resembled a party napkin in his ham-sized hand. Even his voice sounded piggish.

Phil guided his wife until she stood behind his left shoulder, but made no attempt to confront the guy.

Here stood a poster boy for the die-hard supporters, Nixon's silent majority, sprinkled among the waiting—the kind of person who perceives insult in every opinion and takes them as calls to violence; the kind who carries grudges to the grave, not too different from old Milhous. Taking everything personally had won Nixon the presidency, then lost it.

Porky looked ready to fight.

Carol, of course, jumped at the chance to attack Nixon's legacy. "Why?" she stepped out from behind her husband and away from the line until everyone could see her. "To see him dead. To curse his memory. He was a national disgrace. An American embarrassment. An evil, evil man, who hurt innocent people and shamed our country." When she saw that she'd angered Porky further, she gave the point of her comment a twist. "A con man and a psychopath."

"Listen, missy. Somebody ought to teach you some respect. Both of you."

Phil just stood, scared shitless by the threat.

"Go to hell, redneck!" She flipped him off, too, before Phil could pin her arm down.

The man stepped out of line and started to come towards them. He was big, but mostly fat—his shorts were so tight that his thighs bulged out at the bottoms—and not really menacing. He couldn't move well. Phil shouldn't have been afraid—face him down and the guy would probably mouth off but not do anything. There were cops watching and sooner or later one of them would notice the commotion. But Phil turned to stone. Too scared to handle the challenge and too scared to run away, because if he did Carol would give it to him worse when they got home.

I cut the guy off.

"They're with me," I said.

"Our friends." Mina stood by my side. "And they won't disrespect the President again. We won't let them."

I hadn't seen her come over. She was close enough for me to put an arm around her waist, the way we used to stand in line for concerts and ballgames.

"They shouldn't even be here," he said. "Goddamn hippies. They're everything that's wrong with this country."

I could sense Phil restraining his wife. "Just let it go, mister." I stood, hands on hips, like a bouncer. "All that's gonna happen is that we'll get kicked off the line. You don't want that and I... we don't want that." How many other confrontations were occurring in the miles of people ahead of us?

The man became red-faced, which added to his barnyard demeanor, but when no one else backed him up, he returned to his place, lurching and mumbling all the way. I felt proud that I'd handled the threat for them.

We turned around and saw Phil waving a dozen or so mourners ahead of them, to put more distance between us and the man.

"I don't know," I said. "How're we going to keep her from

mouthing off for the next few hours? We may never make it to the viewing. This crowd might string us up."

Mina ducked back into our original place in line, and she grabbed my sleeve to pull me in too. "I don't want to stand with them anyway," she said. She was looking at the sunset now, which glowed like a lit cigarette through the LA smog to the west, and I looked at her.

She'd lost a few pounds. Her jeans fit like a model's, like they'd been designed for her ass alone. I'd noticed when we picked her up that she'd had her hair cut shorter, the way I'd suggested a few times and which she said she'd never do. Maybe Rob liked short hair too.

I always thought married people got heavier right away, from less time working out and more time eating and lounging with each other. A goal achieved, marriage meant the singles regimen could be discarded in favor of nuzzling in front of the TV, alternating kisses with cookies and wine. But Mina looked as though she'd gone hardcore on the aerobics she did occasionally when we went out, like she had something still to prove.

"Nice thing you did there," I said.

"What?"

"Standing up to that guy with me."

I'm not sure she would have done that while we dated. She'd always defined men's and women's roles pretty clearly, and men held the responsibility of handling confrontation.

"It was the right thing to do," she said.

I hid my confusion in an attempt to compliment. "No doubt you could have handled him by yourself."

She smiled at last. "No doubt." The dusk made it harder to see, but I know she flexed to prove her point. The refined geometry of her body triggered erotic fantasies, although the real memories of our relationship didn't look like that. We'd been comfortable, not so much passionate, a grownup version of house that I wasn't ready to play. Still, in the months since we split I'd missed her, maybe out of loneliness or maybe because the reward of middle class values—marriage, career, kids, futility—was the only existence I'd been schooled in.

Years before, Nixon's blatant evils had begun to devalue that still life for me. I listened to the radio broadcasts of the Watergate hearings in my old Ford in the high school parking lot. While the other students cut class for cigarettes and makeouts, I sat transfixed by Senator Sam and the parade of denials that amounted to testimony in the president's defense. The details of the crimes resisted like a stubborn, decayed tooth, and although I didn't know quite what it all meant, I knew it was more important than the other kids' top forty.

Phil interrupted my thoughts about making a comeback with Mina. "Hey, what are you guys doing up here? Come join us." He stood next to us, laughing, the fool's attempt at saving face.

"This is where we were," Mina said. "You moved."

"And that's where we are…" Phil pointed to Carol, who had her hands on her hips. I would've bet she sent him up to fetch us.

"We're good here," I said. "Moving back will probably cost us another ten minutes."

"What's ten minutes when you're waiting ten hours?"

Carol had had enough too, and came forward. "Just get in line Phil," she said, pushing him in. "I'll protect you."

Mina cracked up. I would have too if it hadn't been so pathetic. Porky watched the whole scene, sneering the entire time. What could I do but shrug my shoulders at him?

None of us spoke for a good hour, and in that time we moved a few hundred feet, which seemed like hardly at all, since the line still extended farther than any of us could see. The crowd quieted as well, as night closed in and the drop in temperature brought out jackets and sweaters. The full moon brushed the queue like an artist's wash. Ironic that Nixon would go out with such a celestial blessing. I thought about mentioning it to Carol, but anticipated her response and decided against it. Mina stayed close, and a couple of times I thought she might rest her head on my shoulder. I would have liked that, but then I'd have to fight the urge to hold her like the old days. We jostled against each other two or three times as the line shuffled, but she didn't acknowledge the contact, didn't offer anything like an encouraging look. If I'd played our relationship right the first time around, things would be different now. I wanted another chance, the hell with the current situation.

I reached for Mina, but continued silence was not Carol's thing, and her new outburst stopped me. "So you really thought the bastard was a good president?" she asked. The détente between her and Mina had to end. I was surprised she'd let it go on so long.

"There's a lot more to it than Watergate," Mina said. "Sure, he made his mistakes. But he was what the country needed."

They kept their volume down this time, in deference to any more lunatics in the crowd, but this did not placate Phil, who monitored the line, on the lookout for danger. When I noticed him, he pawed at the ground, finally feeling the embarrassment of his non-performance earlier.

"He broke the law," Carol said. "Even the president isn't above the law."

"What law? Exactly what crime did he commit?" Mina asked.

That one had always been a little murky to me, too.

"There was the break in," Carol said.

"Which he didn't order."

"The cover up."

"All for the protection of his office. The presidency is too important."

Mina was heading for the shelter of executive privilege—Nixon's defense—and that would have opened up an entirely new debate, one that Porky and the rest of the crowd might liked to have joined. She seemed excited now, the way she'd been when we first started dating. And we had plenty of time to talk about it. The queue had come to another of its standstills, as though a couple of miles down the road, at the Presidential Library, they'd decided to close the doors to the viewing and send the rest of the people home. We had no way to know what went on up there. The government was in charge and that meant we were sure to be kept in the dark, and probably lied to.

"His biggest crime was in destroying our trust," Carol said. "Ever since, we can't believe in our president." She looked confident this statement could not be trumped.

"I trusted him," Mina said.

I had no doubt about that. Mina believed the things Nixon said, in the same way she idolized her father and quoted his little maxims from time to time, those nuggets of homespun illogic that always irritated me. She believed the claims made in TV commercials and the fake humility of celebrities and professional athletes. She went to church with her mother on Sundays and trusted what the pastor said the Bible meant.

She trusted me, for a while.

It had been a bull session, one of those after work gatherings, six exhausted and frustrated swing shift auto workers, hot to pound beers and rip management for being the clueless toadies we knew they were, although we also knew the execs were just people we might have become ourselves if we'd had the schooling and the drive. But this time Roger's sister had come home from college, and she joined the group, drunk before we got there and wearing a tank top with no bra. The guys surrounded her like hyenas tracking a gazelle. And for whatever reason, she picked me to flirt with, maybe because I was taken and was the only one not hitting on her with come-ons and posturing straight from the boys' locker room.

How could a guy turn that down? And it would have been the perfect one nighter, both of us so trashed we wouldn't even remember the other's name the next day. All sex and no remorse, a weekend in Vegas right here at home. Except somewhere in the clinches she asked me about my girlfriend, and I started talking. What I liked about her. What I didn't like. Danni—maybe that was her name—asked me about what we did in bed, and I couldn't stop myself I was so shitfaced, and I went on about how Mina was too straight-laced, inexperienced, and that I would appreciate a woman who knew what a man wanted, like someone had opened a tap and said it was okay to let my stupid hang-ups pour out.

I felt like a crook ratting on myself, but I couldn't stop.

Still, I thought no harm would come of it. The night would settle into a fine memory. But instead of going back to school after her break, Danni bailed on college and moved in with her brother. When Mina and I came over a week later, she sat there—cutoffs, tank top and sex drive, and a mouth that couldn't be controlled, and when I acted like she didn't exist, Danni played back everything I'd said about Mina like Nixon's eighteen minutes had been found and broadcast on the nightly news. Mina got Roger to drive her home and she dumped me on my answering machine. We didn't speak again until I called tonight. If some psychiatrist studied our case and said my actions were intentional, that I had done it out of some subconscious fear of confinement, or maybe paranoia, I would have believed it.

Looking at Mina now, knowing that she left her new husband to drive all this way with me, I wanted to think she'd buried that awkward time and was ready to reevaluate our relationship, starting over at least as friends, maybe more.

She touched my hand before she spoke. Her fingers felt cold. "What if it gets to be like two or three in the morning and we still haven't gotten to the viewing?" she asked.

"There's a pretty good chance of that," I said. "Maybe we could bribe someone way up ahead to let us in."

"You'd have to bribe about a thousand people," Carol said. "Anyone who saw you sneaking into the line would be pissed."

"It was a joke, Carol." Her antagonism drained me. She never let anyone slide from her moral judgments. Why I hadn't become sick of it before puzzled me. Maybe I'd been nice to her because Phil was my friend, but now, after his pitiable show, even our friendship was on the table.

I turned to Mina. "You think you have to get back?"

"I wrote Rob a note. I said I'd be home by midnight at the latest."

It was almost eleven. If we headed for the car now she still wouldn't make it on time. She'd wanted to be married, and now she was, and I suspected she was the one chafing at commitment now.

"You should stay. See it out. You'll never have a chance like this again."

"I think I should go."

"Maybe you could call him."

"Where's a phone? Do you have one?"

"Maybe Porky does. Phil could ask him."

Carol didn't like that joke either. "Fuck off, Tyler," she said. She spoke to me, but glared at Phil. An old feeling snaked through me—the one that says when a woman decides her man isn't enough of a man, there isn't much he can do to change the perception.

Nixon was paranoid. That was the consensus. The most powerful man in the world, so scared he might lose power that he risked his office to bug a campaign that had no chance of beating him in the election. He'd been so smart about China and Russia—met them on their turf, opened channels, agreed to discuss differences, found common ground in an effort to avoid hostilities—but when it came to his own country, he didn't trust anything to work out in his favor. Before he became president he thought the media had treated him unfairly—the voters too. He knew too well how politics really worked, and knew the system wouldn't serve his interests, because it wasn't set up to do that. So he didn't think twice about deceiving the public. How many tyrants see it that way, and try to skirt their countries' laws until freedom goes underground, all the while telling the population how much better they are that they're in charge? The insanity is that he thought he could get away with it—that's always the insanity—or that he didn't think about the possibility of discovery at all. But once the media figured it out, Nixon didn't last eighteen months, halfway through his second term.

I gave Carol and Phil six months.

That would still be longer than Mina and Rob would last. And then, of all the relationships, Mina's and mine would have lasted the longest.

Mina looked at Carol. Instead of animosity, I saw a connection between them, a mutual sympathy, as though they understood each other's problems with their men without having to speak a word.

"I'd really like to get going now," Mina said. "I can't stay all night."

"Yeah," Carol said. "Neither can we." Phil moved to put his arm around her shoulder, but she took a step away from him. "Go get the car," she said, and he didn't argue, just reached into his pocket for the keys and pulled them out, and then looked back at where we'd come from, trying to remember the way.

He took a couple of steps, and Mina said, "Wait. I feel like walking. I don't want to just stand here. Can't we go with him?"

"All right," Carol said.

They started to leave, but when they saw me not moving they stopped.

"Come on," Mina said. "We're going."

"You guys go ahead."

"You want us to come get you?"

The line moved another ten feet. I took a look at Porky, who waddled when he walked. The flag he'd carried was no longer in his hand, but hanging limp from his back pocket, on the verge of falling out.

"No. Go without me. I want to see him."

"How the hell are you going to get home?" Carol asked.

Phil's eyes pleaded with me to come. He didn't want to drive alone with these two on the trip back.

"Beats me," I said. "Maybe Porky'll give me a ride."

Carol rolled her eyes.

"We can't just leave you," Mina said.

"Why not?"

"It wouldn't be right."

I was going to say that I didn't mind, that I would be okay and that they shouldn't worry because I was a big boy and could take care of myself. But that might have sounded like another shot against Phil. So instead I said, "What would be right?"

Which didn't make sense to any of them, and they stared at me like maybe I'd gone crazy in the last ten seconds.

I answered for them. "Right is whatever you believe in, if you believe it strongly enough," I said.

I guess they felt sure then that I'd gone crazy, and the two women started walking. Carol didn't bother to turn around, but yelled, "Phil! Let's go!"

He blinked at me and held his hand up in a weak goodbye. Then he took off after them.

When Nixon left office, on that last, hot day in August, he stopped on the steps to the presidential chopper, turned and saluted the crowd and the TV cameras. In his shame he had the guts to smile, like it wasn't really happening, like he was already planning another of his returns to public life. He'd go back home to SoCal for a while, let the nation's anger dissipate, then come back, once more, in honor, as he had so many times before. People just needed time to realize his decisions, his actions were right; time to create new perspectives, whether they're true or not.

I looked straight up to notice a dozen or so stars, faint in the night sky. The atmosphere in southern California holds so much pollution we only get to see about a tenth of what floats out there in space, and for a minute I imagined a sky the ancients might have seen, so brilliant with lights and mysteries they understood themselves to be but a tiny part of the universe. Sometimes we forget what we can't see, and then we believe it was never there.

I scanned the line in front of me as it began to move again. Each time we advanced people became solemn, halting their conversations as though imagining what they would see at the end of their vigil: the hunched body laid straight in the coffin, that dour face that hid so many secrets, the eternal five o'clock shadow that no pancake makeup could cure. I determined I would wait with them—all night and into the morning until I saw him, this man, this great pathetic man, who had come back to be buried among his people.

Caging the Butterfly

If she brought a cup of poison to me, I would drink it. I would do anything for my beloved.

She stands in the doorway to my bedroom and asks if I want bourbon in my milk. The glass is in her left hand, the flask in the other, and her raised arms pull her robe open to reveal a negligee in which I may not indulge. Muffled noises emanate from behind her, in the gloom of the hallway—bare feet creaking the hardwood. Urgent, deep breaths.

"Bring them to me," I say. "I can't sleep well without them."

She pours a little of the whiskey into the milk and leaves both on my nightstand.

"Martine! Will you sit with me until I fall asleep?"

She looks at me quizzically while her impatience simmers. I was the one who insisted Philip stay with us. It only makes sense, I explained, for lovely Martine's personal trainer to be available whenever she needs him.

"It will just be for a few minutes. If you could hold my hand."

She sits on the edge of the bed and grazes my fingers with hers, just barely touching, as if the burlap of my skin sickens her. When she leans forward her hair slips over her shoulder and settles in front of her breast. I want to reach up, brush her tresses to the side like opening a curtain, and stroke her body. I do not move, yet she jerks herself away, reading my thoughts.

What sort of creature does she see? I am reflected in the black of her eyes, my face like parchment, ready to crumble and fall away. If only I could leap through that portal, into another dimension—then it would be me in the hallway instead of him, ready to make love to her.

How I have deluded myself over the years.

Martine is anxious to leave. Her evening is just beginning while mine comes to its end. "One minute more," I say, but I am not sure she hears. She seems to be anywhere but with me. No matter. The alcohol soon makes my eyelids heavy. I nod off for a few seconds, then shake myself awake, but my consciousness won't last long. I tell her she may go, and she pivots from the bed without a word or even a nod. She is a child turned loose into a playground, and I am too weak to rebuke her for the lack of manners.

Martine clicks the door shut. She knows I don't like it closed, but I am a moment from sleep and can't get up to open it.

A storm congeals outside. The wind bangs against my window. It blows so hard the beams and walls of the old house groan, as if complaining about years of neglect. It's not for lack of money. I simply haven't cared. Somewhere in the distance thunder echoes my lament.

I plant a suggestion in my mind to dream about my love and close my eyes again, knowing morning will come soon enough, and the sins of the night will have passed.

I rise early and struggle from the bed. I unlock her door and creep to the chair at Martine's bedside, so I may watch her. Some days she doesn't awaken for hours, and I stay the entire time, marveling as she stretches and turns, mesmerized by the emotions she displays in sleep, the smiles and grimaces, the pleasure and distress of her dreams. I don't worry about Philip, that bulging idiot, intruding. He has his orders, his own interests to protect. He knows I don't want to find him in her room when I enter.

How unlike her father she is, fit and lithe, golden from the life I have afforded her, careful about every nuance of her appearance, spending all morning to perfect her hair and face. She is as beautiful as he is ugly, as desirable as he is repulsive. All the more reason to be proud I captured this butterfly from the chrysalis he wove. She was his starlet, his treasure. Dechambeau must curse me every day. Let him. We are still far from even.

There is one connection between them, father and daughter, but it's nothing physical. The seed of his evil stirs in her heart, waiting to grow, to engulf and choke her like ivy. It must be cultivated. I already sense contempt behind her emotions. I see it in her scowl when I force her to converse, even if I include Philip in the discussion.

I've infringed on their fun often lately, insisting the three of us go to dinner or a concert. I sit between them, claiming her, as is my right, and pretending ignorance of their affair, as they must do to continue my largesse. Their sexual squirming amuses and intrigues me. It's been so long I almost don't remember the feeling, but still I enjoy watching them perform.

Today Martine opens her eyes at a decent hour, but she offers less forgiveness for my intrusion than usual.

"Do you have to sit here every morning, Charles?"

"You are my wife," I remind her. "God knows we have nothing else that resembles a marriage. Grant me this small indulgence."

"It frightens me. I don't like being watched like that."

"You don't need to worry," I say. "Honestly, what could this ancient body do to one so young and strong? Besides, you are watched wherever you go. A woman of your beauty must feel the stares of admirers everywhere."

Still, she seems uncomfortable that her husband is her voyeur. She slips into her robe before she gets out of bed, and runs into her bathroom to pout. I will have to do something nice for her today—perhaps another outfit or some jewelry. It's amazing that she doesn't tire of such things, but then, each of us has an object that never fails to thrill: she has her looks, Philip has his muscles, and I have Dechambeau.

I still remember the note—every word. They would arrive in Majorca before I read it. Elaine seemed so sad that she'd kept everything from me—the affair, the travel plans, how Dechambeau helped her withdraw the funds from our accounts.

"I still love you," she wrote. "But I must go with Marcel. He rules my soul and I am powerless to refuse him."

And beneath her signature, without her knowledge I'm sure, this, in Dechambeau's scrawl: "When we get to Spain we'll toast to Othello." His actor's way of goading me, of plunging the dagger a little deeper, to gouge my heart with this cuckoldry. I despised his oily smile from the first; his way of pumping my hands as he begged for donations for the derelict stage he dared call a playhouse. But Elaine loved the little theater. She encouraged him. Her performance, not his, blinded me.

He sent me photos in the mail every few weeks as they toured, to keep the wound fresh. The first were merely shots of them in their hotel lobby. Later he sent candids from the nude beach at Ibiza—the two of them lying together in the sand like sea turtles.

I hired detectives, tried to track them down through relatives and friends, but they simply abandoned everything they'd known here. They had my money, and they could make new friends and opportunities with it.

I didn't learn he'd killed her until months after it happened.

He'd been so drunk he came out of the wreck unhurt. Of course he fled the country to avoid arrest. It took me another half year to find out where she was buried.

Martine has a picture of him on her dresser, and it is all the reminder I need. He writes to her, asking, I'm sure, why she stays with me. When I consider what he's done I become cold, hateful. No one could blame me for thinking of revenge.

While they play tennis the good doctor visits me in my room. "Weintraub, I am not going anywhere," I say. "What would it give me, another three months?"

He recites the chants of the physicians' religion. Their voodoo. "If you'll just check yourself in," he says, "we can treat this disease properly. We have new drugs, new techniques that show promise…"

…in laboratory rats, no doubt. I suspect my possible recovery has more to do with Weintraub's reputation than my well being. Doesn't my quality of life count for anything? Does he really think I want go through the torture of surgery just to haunt this house a little longer, drag myself through musty passageways and listen to Martine and Philip rut like elk behind the door of every empty room, day after day? Let me go, I tell him. Just make it as painless as possible. He hands me a vial of pills, but I am not done with him.

"I want something else. Something that will let me be with Martine."

"I can't give you that," he says. "Your heart's in no condition for sex."

"I'm dying anyway, Weintraub. What difference does it make how I go?"

He resists me, but I won't let him leave until I have my way. I remind him of the donations I've made to his hospital, the wing that bears Elaine's and my name. He doesn't put up much of a fight. Doctors want to prescribe. It's their duty to help the sick. He chastises himself as he gives me the paper, but I ignore him. Then I send him on his way as if he were a delivery boy.

When he's gone I shuffle down to the court to watch my two children. The cracks in the cement make it difficult to play, and Martine's frustration shows. Like the house, I've let it deteriorate to the point where it's not worth repairing.

He is letting her win, again, as if she wouldn't submit to him tonight unless he did. Really, Philip, you accommodate her too much. Do you think she would turn you away? Consider her alternative. This ravaged shell instead of you?

She doesn't realize my condition is more than old age, not that she cares enough even to ask, but I have sworn Weintraub to silence. I wouldn't want her feeling sorry for me. Before they can finish their game I call to Philip. I want a Le Pin to go with tonight's dinner. He must leave now if he's to get it before the wine shop in town closes.

Martine slams her racket to the court. "Why can't the driver go and get it?"

"Because Nathan is so dumb he'll bring back the wrong thing. Philip isn't as stupid as that one."

Her father's malice shows through her glare. Philip tells her it's all right and jogs inside to get the keys. I join him and slip the prescription into his hand. He is clearly impressed. "Good for you, sir," he says. It almost makes me smile.

Sometimes at night, Elaine comes to me. She begs me to leave the poor girl alone. "It's you I love," I tell her. "I never would have even spoken to her if you hadn't left me."

"You must forget about me," Elaine says. "She is your wife now, and you have a responsibility."

It has to be my mind, playing tricks. I never intended for Martine to care for me, only to marry me. The anonymous roses and gifts of jewelry provided the bait. I paid a poet to compose the letters I sent. Then, the house and cars did their work. They, and the financial papers I left in plain sight became the net. Still, it took more than a year before she would even consider a relationship. Dechambeau tried to keep her from me. He told her lies; he told her the truth. He pleaded like a child. But I knew she shared his avarice, and that she could not resist.

"No strings," I told her. "I only want company in my declining days. Something pretty to look at from my rocker. She said at least I had a fair sense of humor.

Then the hook: "And everything I have will be yours." More of a business proposition than a romance. I showed her the will. Had it witnessed by the attorneys.

But still she wouldn't commit. "It's the sex, isn't it?" I asked. "The thought of me with you, inside you. Am I that revolting?"

She looked at the ground, fighting to keep from tipping her greed.

"Give me our wedding night," I said. "After that I won't bother you, and you'll be free to spend my money." A quiet wedding in Big Sur. A cabin overlooking the Pacific. And of all the ironies, my age forbidding consummation. She laughed, turning the joke into insult, the reverse of what her father did. Which is more painful I cannot say. And whatever doubts I had about her were erased in those first hours.

Still, I've always thought she should give me another chance.

When we returned to the house we set up separate bedrooms. Two weeks later I gave Philip to her as a belated nuptial gift, and explained he would serve as her trainer, and if she preferred, my stunt double. I wouldn't even need to watch.

No, Elaine, there is nothing between us. How could there be? At night she rests across the hall in Philip's arms, and instead of jealousies I think of you, how we lay together in the tall grass behind your family's estate, mapping the stars, exploring the textures of each other's bodies, wanting never to move from that spot, knowing our lives could never improve on that moment.

Did Dechambeau win you with gifts, or promises of some ethereal love? Was it because he was younger and more capable? I know he must have assaulted me, heaped lie upon lie until you suspected my devotion. Still, I can't bear to believe you found something to desire in that scheming con man. Or perhaps your beauty and gentleness softened him, gave him the resolve to charade as something other than the monster he is.

I'm sure you learned the truth of him before you died, before he murdered you. That's why your spirit cannot rest, but instead haunts my mind, seeking relief from your guilt. You tell me to love Martine, as if that is the way you will find peace. But I have another solution.

I made sure to send Philip for a vintage they couldn't possibly have in stock. He's really quite diligent—hates to disappoint me. Always compliant as well. Sometimes, in my less sober moments, I imagine him as the son Elaine and I could have had. He'll be gone for hours, arguing with the owner rather than risking my wrath, then trying other shops to see if they can help. I can see him in the supermarket, searching among the macaroni and cheese for a thousand dollar Pomerol. It will give Martine and me a chance to become reacquainted. "I want to talk with you," I say, "without Philip flexing his ignorance."

She hesitates, like a child about to be admonished. I smile to put her at ease. "Weintraub says I could last another ten years," I say. "In case you were wondering about your future."

She looks at me the way a cat stares at a bird through a window —malicious thoughts tempered by lack of opportunity.

"He gave me a prescription to enhance our marriage. I've been thinking about our agreement."

I have her attention. "You promised," she says. "I'm only supposed to comfort you."

"There are different types of comfort."

"You're too old for that. Too weak."

"That was before I had Weintraub's blessing. And his vial of miracles."

She seems to be searching for a way out of my proposition. But she knows what refusal means.

I offer a solution: "You can always imagine I'm Philip."

"You could never be Philip. Look at yourself—bent and shriveled, like a disease. I can't even look at your face with all its spots."

"I'm hurt, Martine. You must know that I wasn't always this way."

"Even in your youth, in your best days, you could never hope to be him."

"You love him?"

"Yes."

"You would leave me for him?"

She is silent, pouting. Even at this young age she is intelligent enough to realize my money means a life without concern, a future of possibilities. Philip too, his muscle-bound brain operating at the level of an ox's, already knows.

"No," she says at last.

We both know what it means. The charade continues.

Later, Philip returns with a dozen excuses, a small white bag, and a case of fine wines, obviously hand selected by the shop owner to help him placate me.

"You poor boy. I must be getting senile," I say while I take the vial out of the bag. "I never intended for you to spend so much time because of my mistake. You didn't have to go to this much trouble for me."

"It was no trouble, sir. I am happy to do it."

Martine looks as though she wants to punch him.

While she continues to steam, a wave of pain clenches my

chest. My heart, ignored for too long, announces itself and I brace against the table. It means to play a part in this drama.

"You should rest," Martine says. "Just sleep tonight and you'll feel better in the morning."

"I intend on feeling better sooner than that." I turn to go, but stop at the entrance to the dining room and shake the container of magic. "I will see you in my room at eight." If I can make it to the stairs without her seeing the extent of my pain, she will have nothing to suspect. Martine will rant to him about this new bargain I've imposed, and when the moment presents, he will broach a solution in the guise of an idle thought. He is more obedient than even she suspects.

I wait for her on the bed, in my robe and nothing else. The pills—both kinds—have done their job. She enters, a few minutes late, closes the door behind her, but holds on to the knob.

"Come closer, Martine."

"Philip is outside," she says. "If I call to him he'll come in."

"You won't call."

"He won't let you hurt me."

"The furthest thing from my mind," I say. "But if he wants to listen to the fun, he's welcome. He's a good boy, after all. I trust him."

"Why do you hate us?"

"It is not that. Not that at all."

She hasn't moved since she came in. I see her face is contorted in fear and disgust. Can I be so horrible? I am to her what Dechambeau is to me. But this anguish on her part is, unfortunately, necessary. "Please," I say. "I will be gentle." Hatred for her and Philip has nothing to do with it. In fact, their feelings don't factor in at all. I am an old man, who has lived the last thirty years of his life in the purgatory of a wife stolen and murdered, condemned to a loneliness only the deepest love can cause.

Nothing else mattered to me for decades.

Then, at last, I came to know my life was nearly over, and I had spent most of it pining for the woman who abandoned me. I had means, and thought to use them to make my last few months bearable. Tonight is merely an exercise, to see if I can enjoy something of humanity, perhaps for the last time.

"Take off your clothes, Martine," I say. "Lay on the bed and close your eyes. You are my wife."

She sits next to me. With her eyelids pressed shut she begins to unbutton her blouse. She uses one hand, and it takes forever to remove the garment. I help her slide it off her shoulders, and touch her bare skin with my fingers. They are cold and she twitches at their icy feel. "I'm sorry," I say, and experience a moment of remorse. But it passes.

She is smooth and sensual, and I cannot help but rest my head against her breast.

I take a breath, and indulge in the intoxication of her body. "Elaine," I say, "I knew you would come back to me."

"Philip!" Martine cries. She pulls away. Her eyes are wide open now, and I see her fear has turned to horror.

The brute charges through the door, but stops. He's not ready to risk everything I mean to him. Instead of attacking me, he pulls Martine close to him. In his insect's mind he thinks this display will satisfy her without alienating me.

Martine rages, "I can't go through with this." But immediately she realizes the jeopardy in which she's placed her future and begins to retract. "Not yet. I need to think about this. Maybe tomorrow or in a couple of days. It's all happened so fast."

Martine, get my newspaper from the den. Bring me a bourbon, straight up. No, I don't want Philip to do it. I want you.

She confronts me. Claims she won't stand for this treatment. She is not a slave.

"It's time you became more of a wife," I say, "and if you can't perform your bedroom duties, I can invent other ways to fulfill our agreement. Think of it as a job and remember all the money these menial tasks will be worth when I finally die. Not exactly minimum wage work."

"You are evil," she says.

"And for now, while I am still here, I won't be as generous with my resources. At least not as long as you remain so distant."

"Then I will get a divorce."

"A good idea. You'll get a few thousand dollars and you will be rid of me."

"I'll get more than that. I'm half of this marriage. I'll take at least that much. More because of all the pain and suffering you've caused me."

"Yes," I say. "The pain of a Mercedes convertible. The suffering of Vera Wang and Valentino in your closet. You came into this relationship with nothing, and my lawyers will make sure you go out the same way. All my friends have seen the way you carry on with Philip, and they'll be sure to tell the judge. If anything, I should divorce you. Now that's an idea…"

"You wouldn't do that…"

"You are trapped, Martine. Caged in this marriage. The only way out is to see me die, but then, Weintraub said that won't happen for some time, didn't he? Poor Martine."

Philip comes in from his latest errand and Martine runs to him. "Baby," she says, "He's gone insane."

Perhaps I have. What does it matter?

"You have to do something. Make him stop. Make him leave me alone," she says.

"What can I do?" he says. "It's his house. Charles makes the rules."

I say, "Don't count on Philip to rescue you. He's on my side. Aren't you, my boy?"

His silence is the most eloquent thing he's ever said. He is not as stupid as I have made him out to be.

She marches out to the sundeck and he follows.

"Come back," I say. "I need another drink. I need a magazine."

I shouldn't torture the girl, but it is the only way I can get her to see the solution. It will be soon, I pray. My insides shriek with agony. My heart is dying, and even the medication cannot numb all the pain. I'll keep after her every day until she understands, until she agrees to Philip's proposal.

My love for Elaine, my contempt for Dechambeau, sustain me. But at times I wonder if the relationship isn't the other way around. My memory of her fades, the image loses focus. Every recollection leads to the insult of her abandonment. She chose to leave. And Dechambeau—are we not more alike than I want to admit? We loved the same woman, kept the same woman. Had Elaine been his wife, I would have pursued her until she left him. Had Martine been my daughter, would he belittle her, degrade her as I have?

Dear Martine, you are not a slave. You are a pawn.

Philip comes to me while she visits her hair salon. "She is ready," he says. "She made the buy this morning. Aconitine. A single tablet. She showed it to me, and her plans for when you are… I have no wish to remain here in her employ."

"Thank you my boy. You can't know how much I appreciate you."

He smiles. He does know, of course.

At night, with the wind howling outside, the despair of this house is like a crypt. It seems to know, better than we, how hopeless is our future.

She approaches this time without reluctance. I've given her no choice. She wears that negligee again and poses to show she's finally ready for me. She asks if I want her to massage my back first. It will be relaxing and sensual, she says.

"You seductress. How could I resist?"

She has the pill hidden in her bra. So tempting. A tug of the elastic, and it tumbles, tiny and blue, from her lingerie into her hand. I only catch a glimpse, but I can see the difference.

"Let me," she says, and slides it into my mouth, then hands me the bourbon to wash it down.

"It will be a few minutes," I say.

Martine crosses the room and sits in the faded Louis XV, clasping her thighs together as though locking them. "It will be forever," she says. She seems nervous. I don't blame her.

"What a sweet sentiment. I may feel something for you after all."

"What do you mean?"

"Before I go. The pill was poison, wasn't it?"

She stands and puts her hand to her throat. "How do you know?"

"Philip knows. And when he knows, I know." Yes, I can sense the chemicals working. The pain in my body relaxes. My mind begins to spin. "How did you get it? It wasn't Weintraub, I hope. I'd hate to see him complicit."

"It doesn't matter. I'll say you had a heart attack trying to have sex. You will be dead and Philip and I will have everything. You won't be missed—not by anyone."

"That may be true," I say, "But he might have at least a touch of sadness from time to time."

Philip pushes the door open and comes to the bed. He checks my pulse. His manner is calm and professional, like a doctor's. Martine doesn't understand, and stares at him as if he were a stranger. Now who looks stupid?

I don't have much time. I feel the poison racing through me, carrying me to my beloved. But time enough to revel. "The greedy are easily recruited to a cause, my dear, as you know. Philip is mine. He'll be my witness. It's he who will have everything."

Martine tries to pretend I am only rambling, but the panic of realization is in her eyes. I hear appeals to their love, to the logic of a future together. She pleads with him not to turn her in. Claims she's too young to go to prison. But the terms of the new will are clear. He gets everything, but only if…

A tree branch scrapes its fingernails against my window. The house lets out a groan that seems like a sigh. My body quakes and seizes. I have imprisoned the butterfly. I strain to see her anguish, but there is only darkness. Her voice fades into nothingness. Dechambeau! You took my beloved, and now, at last, I take yours. Remember, every day of your miserable life, that she suffers for you, that she serves your sentence.

Excerpts from the Diary of the Last Emperor of Rome

Archeologists working in the fields near Ravenna, Italy, have recently discovered fragments of writing that appear to be the diary of Romulus Augustulus, generally acknowledged as the last emperor of Rome. Little had been previously known about Augustulus, except that he was probably sixteen or seventeen years old, and that his father, the Roman general Orestes, deposed the sitting emperor, but installed his son on the throne instead of taking it himself. The following excerpts date from August and September in the year 476.

17 August

Septimus advised me to kill the messenger and send his bloody head back to the rebel generals. They'll learn we don't negotiate with thugs, he said. I didn't know what to do, because I had already told the messenger I would grant an audience. Septimus laughed when I told him. They are barbarians, he said. The whole army is nothing but barbarians now. We owe them nothing, not even our word. We'll dismiss them and recruit others. The men in the provinces are dying to come to Italy, he said, and he laughed again, at his own joke. Maybe he's right. Our own men are too lazy to fight, but there are hordes of others who would gladly take their place. Even my personal guard is from the wilderness.

O Father, now Septimus will send word to you of my bad judgment. He always finds a way to make me a fool in your eyes.

I do not feel like an emperor. I wear the robe and crown, but Septimus doesn't respect me. None of them do. I hear whispers, laughter in the hallways, and my commands are met with the stares of dumb compliance, the looks that say, yes Caesar, we obey you because we fear your father's power, but you are nothing to us. You are a boy. And when they're out of my sight they indulge themselves in intrigues. They plot to kill me, I know it. I trust no one. And I burn to escape from this place and this responsibility. Father, why did you do it to me?

You said Septimus is wise and I must listen to him, but he is the worst of them. If you knew what he does when you're not around... I've seen him at night in dark corners of the villa, drinking and whoring with those disgusting women from the city. He carries on like a sailor instead of a patrician. He's as vulgar as the barbarians. I could never be like that. It is an insult to everything Roman.

How I wish you were here. You'd waste no time with this business. And the generals would listen to you, because you have the men and weapons to defeat them. That's all they understand—the sword and the spear. But you are days away in Rome, haggling with the Senate.

To be there instead of this backwater! I long for the old city more than ever. Today I thought of the baker's down the hill from our estate. Such wonderful smells. They used to waft up and greet me in the morning before lessons. I would stand at the wall and breathe them in, and watch the citizens on the street below. How delightful, like attending a parade. In Ravenna I'm lucky to see a dozen carts pass by in a day. I am so isolated. My messages to you go unreturned. I'm sure Septimus intercepts them.

Father, I know you made the right decision to move the capitol here, away from the corruption that has ruined Rome, but I so miss the feeling of our home.

But then, if I were in Rome I might never have met Clemencia. She is my goddess. My reason to persist. I must see her again. But I must wait until I can sneak out without Septimus and his spies knowing.

18 August

Even the sight of Septimus sickens me now. Father, how he has changed in the few months since he arrived. His skin is covered with spots. It hangs from his limbs like a lizard's. He has yellow eyes that seep with disease. And when he is not in my sight he haunts me. I can hear his buzzard's rasp in every room. There's no privacy at all.

I waited until he went into town, probably to procure new prostitutes, and called for the generals' messenger. The man was courteous and well-spoken, a fine representative. They may not be the animals Septimus claims.

He explained the generals' request, Father, and I know you would find it reasonable. The men in the army are from many lands. They are not citizens of Rome, he said, but they fight in our name and protect the empire, so shouldn't they have the right to land in Italy? I can't blame them for wanting to stay here. There's certainly nothing good waiting for them back in Gaul and Germania. Perhaps when Rome ruled the provinces things were better, but now that our borders have shrunk back almost to Italy, those places have become a wasteland. I hear the people live like pigs, scratching a living from the dirt with their hands. They pray to trees and rocks instead of the gods. No wonder the soldiers wish to stay in our country. I say give them each a little plot and turn them into farmers. But I'm sure Septimus will disagree. He'll twist my logic until I sound stupid. If you would just come, I could explain it. And how good it would be to see you after all these months.

I agreed to receive their leader, called Odoacer. I will make this ruling on my own, without Septimus's meddling.

20 August

I rode out of the city this morning, to the farm where Clemencia lives with her family. My slave Vectitos, the Gaul, and I dressed as commoners, so we could pass through the streets unknown. Septimus's men are everywhere. I don't see them as much as I feel them.

Father, Clemencia is as pretty as any of the girls from Rome, despite the rags she must wear for clothing. We talked for a while about the weather and crops. She believes I'm a young merchant, interested in her family's harvest. I can't tell her yet I am the emperor. It's too dangerous for both of us. I hid my rank and spoke of my travels throughout the country, and she believed me.

At first she enjoyed my stories of exotic lands. But then she became distant. I asked her what was wrong and she admitted she was jealous of me, and was angry with herself for feeling that way. She said she is trapped on the farm, just a tool to her parents, no more to them than the ox that pulls the plow. She showed me bruises where her father beats her to make her work harder. It is a miserable life. I watched her eyes as she spoke. I saw them fill with remorse. I wanted to sweep her up and take her back to the villa. But who knows what Septimus would do when he found out.

While she shared her secrets with me I took her hand and kissed it. I tried to kiss her lips, but she pulled away. I thought of forcing myself upon her, as I'm sure Septimus forces himself on the young slaves in the household. But she would have thought I was vile. I am vile for thinking of it.

I know it is wrong for me to be in love with a plebeian. It is against every code our family honors. She's lived her entire life on this farm, isolated from culture and education, exiled in ignorance. But to know her as I do, who would not bless our union?

21 August

Odoacer is nothing like you, Father. He's a short man, shorter even than I, but as wide as a bull. His beard and the mane that flows over his neck make him seem even larger. He was sweating in the summer heat and smelled like a stable. Everything about his presence is violent and revolting. He knocked over a candle stand when he entered, and didn't excuse himself. He merely grunted and kept marching towards me until he was breathing onions into my face.

My hands gripped the chair, but I did not look away. An emperor does not show fear. Then he bowed and took my hand. He accepted a cup of wine and drank it almost like a gentleman. He said for one so young I already have the bearing of a great king. He didn't call me Augustulus, like so many others. It's so insulting to be called "little" Augustus.

We spoke cordially for a while, but then Odoacer said his proposal includes he be made a patrician, like you. How was I to respond to that? As if one could ignore your years of culture and training. Men like Odoacer will always be plebeian, barbarian, no matter what their title. There is no comparison between you and he. You are a full head taller, Father. You are meticulous about your appearance, despite spending a life in the country, among soldiers and commoners. You dress in regal clothes, not animal skins, like the general. You rule through respect, not violence. You are an example of what Rome used to be, and what it still might be.

I told him no. You would have been proud of how I stood up to him.

But Odoacer said it only made sense that the general of the army be of noble rank. Generals have always been patricians. To elevate him would restore this tradition. It was not so much for his own glory, he said, but for Rome's. Although I had suspicions I found it hard to argue.

To be safe, I told Odoacer I needed more time. This displeased him. He threw down his cup and exposed his barbarian heritage. He ranted that an emperor would not need more time. I thought he would draw his sword. I signaled to my guards, but they were petrified and did nothing, and I was forced to endure the onslaught like a child being scolded. Finally he left, vowing to come back for my answer. I sent the guards away and when I was alone I shook with fear and shame.

22 August

As soon as it was light I disguised myself and stole away from the grounds with Vectitos. No one saw us leave. I had to get away, to be in the open air before the walls of the villa closed in on me.

I brought my imperial seal and some gold coins that bear my image. We rode to Clemencia's farm, and this time, instead of chancing to meet her in the fields, I rode directly to her house.

I was not prepared for the squalor in which Clemencia lives. The house is barely big enough to roost chickens, yet she lives there with her parents and two younger brothers in the single room. Smoke from the hearth rose through a hole in the roof.

Her mother came out to the walkway and addressed me as boy. Vectitos almost struck her for her impertinence, but I stopped him. He told the woman to summon Clemencia and her father from the fields, and we went inside to get out of the sun.

The place smelled of goats and excrement. We sat on straw, sweltering. I began to talk about Clemencia. She is so beautiful, so pure. She must have been separated at birth from her true place among the upper class, and had been forced to live this life of hardship and labor. If she had to stay here I knew she would turn into a crone like her mother.

Vectitos said I should forget the girl and leave, but I so wanted to see her, and we waited for what must have been an hour in that heat. When she came inside I was again paralyzed by this Venus. She is not a mere woman, not even a patrician. She is a goddess masquerading among peasants. I realized, Father, that this was a test of my courage, and that the gods would reward me for saving one of their own. I had to rescue her.

Her father stood next to her. He was a squat little man with a bald head burned red from his work in the fields. Another who cannot hope to compare to you, Father. I pulled the seal and coins from my purse and placed them on the table. The greedy father, possessed by Laverna, immediately reached to snatch them up, but Vectitos held his wrist. Do you recognize that seal, he said. Do you know the face on these coins? These are the symbols of the emperor, Augustus. This is his seal, he said, taking my hand and slipping the ring onto my finger.

Clemencia's father looked me up and down. He snorted like a swine. He said I was a thief, and had probably stolen these things.

You are a fool, Vectitos said, and he struck the table with his fist.

What is it to us? The father asked. You expect us to believe this boy is our king?

I am your emperor, I shouted. Clemencia looked away, as though I had gone mad. I tried to explain how I had come to power, how you had set it all up for me, Father. But I knew people like these couldn't care less who is running the government. They raise their crops and try to survive. When the tax collectors or soldiers come, they give up the fruits of their work and get nothing in return.

The father said to hell with the emperor, and again he reached for the coins. Vectitos pushed him hard, knocking him into the wall. The man picked up a piece of wood for the fire and swung it as a weapon, back and forth like a club. I cried to Vectitos to let him have the money, but when the father menaced me, my slave pulled his dagger and jabbed it into his ribs. The little man coughed and spit blood. He clutched his side and went down to one knee, and Vectitos, still enraged, plunged the knife into his neck.

Clemencia and her mother fell upon the body in tears. I couldn't blame my man. It was his job to protect me. He grabbed me under the arm and pulled me outside, to the horses. I was in anguish. What pain I'd caused Clemencia! She was sure to suffer. I prayed to Diana for her safety during our ride back and all night in my room. How she will survive without her father I do not know. She and those two little boys cannot work the farm by themselves. I'm afraid the mother will leave the place and take her children away.

Again I ask for your guidance, Father, and again I get no answer.

26 August

I want to go back to Clemencia, but I know she'll reject me. I'm sick with despair, and don't know what to do to win back her heart.

My days are aimless, as dark and cold as the corridors of the villa, as lonely as the throne I sit on all day. The slaves stay outside my chambers unless I call them. Odoacer hasn't come back. Even Septimus keeps his distance. The only sign I have of him is the racket he and those women raise each evening in his quarters. Last night I hid around the corner and watched them. While they fornicated, I imagined being with Clemencia, feeling her soft skin against me, her lips on my lips, her wet eyes gazing into mine. Why must I live this way? I am an emperor in name only; in hell in my own house.

This morning I went to Septimus and asked him to procure one of the women for me.

27 August

At last, news from Father! A courier arrived at midday with a message. But it was not what I expected. It said you hoped I did not make a rash judgment about Odoacer's proposal. It would mean disaster for the empire to allow those men land rights in Italy. You wrote that you dispatched another messenger to the generals, under my name, denying their request.

How could you have known of my talk with Odoacer? It must be Septimus. The treacherous old ogre.

And I'm worried about the second part of your message, Father. You said to beware of Odoacer. When the general receives our denial he might believe he had been crossed. He might advance on Ravenna and try to get his way by force. But then the best news of all. You are leading your troops to the city as quickly as they can march. When you arrive you will destroy Odoacer's army, and I will see Septimus hauled away in chains.

28 August

The girl Septimus brought to me was young and gentle, nothing like the harlots he prefers. He must have suspected it would be my first time. His kind choice makes me wonder if I've misjudged him.

I asked her if I could call her Clemencia, and she said yes. From the side she looked a little like my love. For a while we merely talked—I of the beautiful girl I met outside the city, she of her childhood in Macedonia. What a sad story. It was her own father who sold her into slavery because the family couldn't support all their children.

I could have spent the entire night talking to her, but she said we should consummate our business. She seemed to enjoy her role as my Clemencia, and when she pressed me to the bed I closed my eyes and believed it was her. When I awoke later, she was gone. I decided to go back to the farm, this time in my armor and with a full company, and pledge to provide for Clemencia and her family, to prove my love to her. I will ask her to be my wife. I know you will support me in this, Father. She will be a fine empress.

29 August

Father is dead. I am truly alone.

Odoacer and his men attacked the legion last night. While I lay with the whore, they routed the soldiers and burned the camp, and dragged Father before the barbarian general. The report says that as they spoke, one of those pigs came up behind him and slit his throat, like an animal.

You were my guide, my light, the Apollo of my heaven. You were the perfect symbol of Rome. And like our once great empire you were pulled into the abyss by the scourge that has infested every corner of the world. Father, my grief for you knows no limits. My hunger for revenge fills me. But it isn't possible. Odoacer's troops approach Ravenna as I write this. There aren't enough guards in the city to repel them. They will crush any defense we mount.

My only chance is to flee, to slip out of the city by the route I use to see Clemencia, and head for Rome. Maybe I can persuade the Senate to gather troops for a counterattack.

I must find Septimus to help me make a plan. I've never appreciated his efforts for me. Now I need him more than ever.

2 September

A thousand years of empire weigh down on me. I must remember that Romulus was a boy when he founded Rome, and Augustus was as young as I when he became emperor. They didn't let their age keep them from greatness. But I am powerless. I have nothing to fight with, and must let the fates dictate my future, and that of Rome. Odoacer surrounded the city in only a day and cut off any chance at flight. He brought bands of mercenaries to support his assault, and even the back roads are patrolled. The municipal guards are no match for them. They'll yield the gates in another day at most.

I'm afraid again. I can't find Septimus. The poor man is probably hiding or has been taken captive. I look for wisdom among his assistants, but all I get are the stares of dullards. Without you here, Father, no one knows what to do. Each time I think of what Odoacer did to you my hatred grows.

The gods knew this day would come. They saw it all. They knew Rome would start from nothing, would rise and crush its enemies. They saw how we would wade through the nations of the world and create its greatest empire. And they foretold its end. When Odoacer comes crashing through my doorway, he will surely send me to join you in the underworld, Father. The barbarians will have seized power, and we will no longer be Rome. The empire will be no more. I will be defeated as emperor, and I will have failed as your son. I curse the gods who have chosen me for this pitiful role.

But perhaps I can still prove my courage. Since I cannot escape, I will stay here and fulfill my duty, even if it's for only another day. I will be brave and prepare for martyrdom. I'll bathe and wear my finest robes to meet the barbarian, and I will not flinch before his sword.

I summoned Vectitos and bade him bribe his way back to Clemencia's farm. If I must die, if I'm to spend eternity in the underworld, I want her there with me. I instructed him to take her life, as quickly and painlessly as possible. She will be waiting for me when I arrive in Hades. Then, away from the madness and intrigues of this life, she will know that I love her, and she will love me.

3 September

We are under martial law. Odoacer routed our defenses and the remaining guards ran off. The compound is surrounded. He made his headquarters in a villa not far from here. But his men have been civil. They haven't sacked the city, or even molested the populace. He sent a messenger to say he would meet with me tomorrow. I'm resigned to my end.

Vectitos returned this morning. It was unfortunate, he said, that he had to kill the mother before he could get to Clemencia, but the task was completed. I thought that when I heard Clemencia was dead I would be glad because it meant we would soon spend eternity together. But instead I trembled in my chair. I curled up and wept.

O, the pain I've caused you, my darling! To see your father and mother murdered, and then to have your own life taken by the assassin. But there was no other way. I'm trapped by the fate the gods have written for me. Please understand. I know you will forgive me when we meet again. How I long to see you in the underworld.

I prayed to Proserpina to care for my beloved until I could join her. It will only be a few hours, maybe a day, before we are together.

And as I prayed I realized I was no longer afraid to die. That is why Father insisted I be made emperor. He knew I would eventually find my strength. I will make you proud yet, Father. If I must die, I'll die as you did, with a dignity the barbarians can never hope to achieve.

4 September

Odoacer sat on my throne and made me bow to him. Septimus was with him, and told the barbarian he would advise him about forming a new administration. He is lower than a snake! He even laughed at me and called me a stupid child. He deserves a traitor's death, sentenced to hell, chained to a stone for all time with vultures picking at his liver.

Odoacer raised his hand to pass judgment on me. I looked into his eyes, waiting for the words that would send me to Clemencia and Father. But he didn't condemn me. He said, no, you shall not die. I've grown to like you. You have promise. And you're just a boy. You don't deserve to be killed. Your father fought against me, so he earned his death, but you I will spare.

He exiled me to Misenum, a spit of land overlooking the sea in the west. He said I would live an easy life, but could never leave that place.

I fell to my knees. I begged Odoacer. But I am ready to die, I said.

No, he said. That will not be necessary.

His men dragged me out and threw me into the atrium, in front of the slaves. I knew they were laughing at me behind their cold eyes.

I was spared, yet I am damned. I will live alone, disgraced, never to see my love or my Father. But then, Odoacer had no need to execute me. I hadn't been, and would never be a threat to him. And it would serve him well when the people learned he spared me.

I am a fool. They all knew it, and they let me trick myself into believing my decisions mattered. And now those I love more than myself are dead because of it. Forgive me, Father. Forgive me, darling Clemencia. I did not see the evil my actions would cause. I am lower even than Septimus.

I summoned my new courage and chose the honorable path. Suicide. It was the only way.

But I couldn't. My hand was paralyzed. The blade at my wrist refused to cut. I dropped the knife and sank to the floor. I am still a coward. But what's the difference if I can't send myself to hell? I am already there, in the darkest, most polluted corner of that prison, condemned to an eternity of regret, for the gods will never allow one so vile to forget his crimes, or to find solace with a Father, or a lover.

The diary of Romulus Augustulus ends here. He lived in exile for ten years in a small castle owned by relatives. It is rumored that each night he demanded a different prostitute be brought to him, and that each answer to the name Clemencia. He was murdered by one of them around the age of twenty-seven.

What We Choose to Remember

I: Let each one of you speak the truth... —Ephesians 4:25

The simple metal rhythm of a darbouka wafts from offstage, reverberating against the auditorium walls and quieting the chatty crowd. An instrument of festival, according to the press packet. The drummer quickens the tempo—a hail of fingers evokes images and sensations of the east: men reclining on embroidered cushions, women in hijab, incense and oases. But Johnny Mars resists the sound. He does not want to enjoy the occasion; he does not want to relax. Once, he would have welcomed the exotic notes as an exploration into another world. Now he conjures an angry terrain of bald mountains, men with sparse beards and ragged, loose clothes, carrying automatic weapons loaded with hate. In his head he hears the sound of jihad. He wishes the music would stop, and begins to hum to himself, a futile effort to cover the noise.

The house lights dim and a spotlight washes over a bearded man in a sharkskin suit. He wears sunglasses, but removes them as he approaches the microphone. The man waits for the darbouka to retreat into a softer cadence, and begins his speech with arms spread, as though blessing the audience. "I believe you all know," he says, "how much the world has missed the voice and the incomparable music of Ahmed Ali for these many years."

Mars stops humming and shifts in his seat. He scribbles the speaker's words on the notepad that came with the fact sheets and studio shots, and appends the quote with editorial. "Lies!" he writes, underlining it twice. The world, he corrects, is wise to this PR stunt. No one has missed Ahmed Ali. It's Zan Williams they've come to London to see. He exhales in disapproval as the emcee dabs his forehead with a handkerchief and continues the introduction. His noise catches the attention of a woman a few seats over—the only other guest relegated to the back row of the conference—and she looks at him. Mars stares back for a second. The woman wears her blond hair draped over one shoulder, the way a girlfriend in college used to. He turns away and strains to see over the heads of the journalists given precedence over him.

Don't thirty-five years in the business count for anything? He'd tried to convince a teenager in glasses and a blue pantsuit, who claimed that his name wasn't on the credentials list, that he belonged inside. She acted as though she'd never heard of him, or Zan Williams, and threatened to call security. She wouldn't budge when Mars dropped names from magazines and decades past, and mentioned his weekly column in Pink Toaster. She'd never heard of that either. Mars protested until her supervisor intervened—there were still a few unclaimed seats, why not let him in? Then she handed him a folder of marketing materials, welcomed him as though there had been no argument and politely directed him to the gulag of the last row.

Mars tries to connect with his neighbor. "Damn," he says to her. "You can't see anything from here. Might as well be sitting behind the stage." He pushes his lips into the approximation of a smile.

She stares again for a few seconds, before gathering her papers and purse and making her way to a seat a few rows closer to the stage. Mars watches as she asks about the lone open spot, then sidesteps past retreating knees and toes to squeeze in. What did he say that was so offensive? Was it the way he looks? He notices how hot it is in the room, and pulls at the collar of his denim shirt to let the air cool his neck.

The suit onstage isn't done dispensing hype. He gushes over Ali's new release—his first in nearly thirty years—titled Moon and Star. He describes Ali's recording company and talks of more music to come. He gestures to the curtains behind, which open to a multimedia Ahmed Ali exhibit, including slides of the singer dressed like a mullah, of him leaning against a doorway. Ali gazing pensively into the camera. Ali playing a guitar. Mars has seen these poses a thousand times, studio shots glorifying the musicians he's covered. They are meaningless to him now, but with a backdrop of music from the new CD, they must seem significant to the crowd.

A huge portrait of Ali lingers on the screen as the other images fade. The pitchman applauds. People in the crowd rise and join the euphoria. Mars gets up too, so he can see the ones down in front, the reporters from the Times, Rolling Stone and the other legacy rags, the cream of music criticism, the junta who decide what will be popular each year. They are applauding too, sacrificing their journalists' impartiality before the conference even begins. There is a part of him that wants to be in that first row, laughing and smiling along with them, claiming a percentage of the celebrity. He, as much as anyone, helped Zan Williams achieve stardom. But they've never allowed him access to their circle, never respected what he's written. He belongs down there with them, but they will never admit it.

There are other people he doesn't recognize, perhaps extras tabbed by the marketing company to fill the seats and add to the event's veneer. But he is on to them. He knows they are too young to remember what Zan Williams meant to the world, to its conscience. Certainly they don't understand that having this impostor, this Ahmed Ali, accept their adulation is an insult to the music he believed in.

Finally the singer comes out. He is dressed all in white—loose pants and a jacket with a mandarin collar, sandals on his feet. In place of the clean-shaven face Mars remembers is a beard trimmed in the style of a Muslim cleric. "Of course," he whispers to no one. "He completes the façade with the clothes of a prophet."

Ali walks to the center of the stage, where a dais has been set up. Three more men in beards and dark suits, who look to Mars like Muslim radicals, but are identified as producers and managers, join him. Mars doesn't bother to write their names down. He is too busy watching Ali, looking for traces of the man he used to be. The singer motions for the audience to sit, and they obey. "May the peace of Allah be with you," he says. "Today I rejoice that He has seen fit to allow me to make music again."

But Mars remains standing. He shakes his head. It shouldn't be this easy. There should be an apology first for what he did to his fans three decades ago. For the betrayal of his philosophy, and of his way of life. For how he'd slammed the door of fundamentalism in the faces of the millions who believed in the freedom and brotherhood he preached in song—the fans who had become the artist's disciples, searchers for a mystical truth that seemed to lay just beyond the music's horizon.

Williams said almost nothing about his decision to quit the music business at the time. Just a one-pager mailed to entertainment magazines saying he had canceled his concert tour and was retiring. Had there been a tragedy? An injury to his voice? But his management offered no explanation. When Williams finally granted an interview, he was a different person—aloof and preoccupied. He had taken a new name, a foreigner's name, and gone into seclusion. His past life and his dozens of recordings, he said, had been blasphemy. Those frivolous pursuits were an affront to God. He took a Muslim wife and proclaimed he would devote the rest of his life to study and prayer.

Islam? How could a man so dedicated to peace join a religion steeped in violence? Mars wrote to Williams's agent and record label. He wanted his chance to interview the artist, to ask his questions, but none of them got back to him.

Ali looks as though he is about to speak, but pauses, shading his eyes from the stage lighting and peering in Mars's direction. He smiles for a moment, looking down at the assembly like a king at his subjects, then returns to his rehearsed comments. "I feel wonderful about singing of life in this fragile world once again," he says. "And with my new album I hope to bridge the religious and cultural differences that often divide us."

Mars clenches his fists. A marketing campaign. Politically correct nonsense. No apology, no deference to the past. Why did he expect Ali to say anything different?

He feels the deceit within the words crawl over him, and begins to tremble. There is a truth inside him, pounding to be let free. Mars squints through his wire-rim glasses at the figure in white, trying to control the emotion raging inside. But it has to be released, and he lets his words flow with the vindictiveness of lava. "Then would you say your denouncement of your music and the entertainment industry thirty years ago was a mistake?"

The interruption stuns Ali, and he takes a step back from the microphone. A mountain in a security guard's jacket moves into the row of seats towards Mars. The man sitting at Ali's right pushes himself up and leans into the microphone. "We will have time for questions in a few minutes," he says. "But first Ahmed would like to discuss his new album." The guard comes within a few feet of Mars, and he sits down, folding his arms and turning inward like a scolded child.

II: Follow the inspiration sent unto thee—Yunus, 10:109

The man Ahmed Ali sees through the mist of spotlight is a throwback to another decade, an anachronism—he wears a denim work shirt and Levi's; dangles strands of hair from the middle of his balding head to his shoulders. His clothes aren't so different from the way Ali used to dress when he was performing in the 1970s. He had hair to his shoulders too, a tapestry of curls that cascaded from his head and which reflected the moods of his songs as he performed, bouncing and swaying as if he were underwater. But the years and the discipline of Islam urge a more conservative approach. That this man still wears the uniform of dissenting youth might have been a pleasant surprise to Ali had he not disrupted the conference.

He sees the stranger is an island, isolated in his empty row by distance as well as fashion. Ali watches as the man shrinks into a cocoon of himself, and senses he is troubled by more than just a few words uttered so many years ago. He holds up a hand to the guard to stop him from removing the man. The question was valid. Probably every reporter and critic in the crowd plans to ask some version of it. The departure from public life had been abrupt, and now his return is, he is sure, nearly as surprising. He turns to his producer. "This seems as good a time as any to talk about that," he says.

"Are you certain? We were going to get them excited about the new CD first. Talk about the future, remember?"

Ali turns back to the audience. "I want to answer that question," he says. He watches the journalists in the front row lean forward, into their notepads. "The answer… is no. It was not a mistake. It was the right thing for me to do at the time." He pauses for a second to look over his shoulder at the enormous photo of himself in contemplation still floating on the screen. "I was lost. My life was a waste. I needed to change everything. Perhaps, when

I made the decision not to perform anymore, I was too zealous, too willing to sacrifice for my new life. I may have been too harsh in speaking about my past, but I was not wrong."

Ali looks into the thick of the crowd. The faces are blank, uncomprehending. In his peripheral vision he sees his producer waving at him below the surface of the dais to stop the digression and get back to the script. He nods that he will. But not yet. "I'm not sorry about it," he says, "if you're curious. For a long time I didn't miss making music. Islam has so much to fill the hours. It is like a new morning, awakening me every day to its beauty."

Now the producer has his chin in his hand and is staring at him, his eyes begging. This is just what he had warned about, allowing the press conference to become a referendum on his religion. The reporters continue scribbling away. A couple have their hands up, hoping to sneak more questions in before the scheduled Q and A. Ali puts his palms up to signal they'll have to wait. "As you see, it's pretty easy for me to get sidetracked, especially into something that's so important. We can talk more about this a little later." He looks out again at the man in the back. "I thank you for raising the issue," he calls to him.

He returns to the prepared remarks—about simple songs, by a simple man—music of love and truth. For a moment it sounds much the way he had spoken about his music thirty years ago, but back then it was the search for truth. A subtle difference. There is only one truth now. Ali calls on the marketing expertise he honed on the concert circuit three decades past, and moves smoothly into details about the album release and negotiations for a brief tour. He is excited, he tells the gathering, about the possibilities, although as he says it, he remembers what traveling and performing had done to him before.

It was on his second tour, on the west coast of the states to promote a new release, that the success of his first album mutated. Validation of his music became an illusion of fulfillment. The change was unexpected and confusing. Suddenly, no one disagreed with him. If he wanted a stage light moved, it was moved. Adjustments in the show's arrangements weren't disputed. He was always right. If he needed a joint before the show, someone brought one to him. Women waited for him backstage, and he took them—two, even three at a time into his hotel room, and later opened the doors and paid for enough wine and acid for a roomful of people—acquaintances and strangers—to last the entire night. When the others finally left he continued the revels by himself, substituting cocaine and heroin for companionship. It felt like falling from a place so high he could never hit the ground, a mind-blowing rush through a cosmic wormhole, transporting him from the struggles of his early career into a new dimension of himself. His friends and his fans melded into shapes indistinct from each other. Whether they existed or not no longer mattered. Days and weeks had no meaning. There were entire concerts he could not remember.

The thought of it now disgusts him. He is grateful to God for the chance to rescue his life. As Ali speaks, he looks sideways at his producer—this conference, and the comeback tour, were his idea. He would have preferred to stay in the studio, away from the scrutiny.

III: Do not let the sun go down on your anger—Ephesians 4:26

When the advance copy of Moon and Star arrived at Pink Toaster it went where all the unwanted submissions went—on the counter next to the coffee maker and paper cups in the break room. Mars made his once-a-week visit to the office and couldn't believe it hadn't gone directly to the magazine's regular music critic, or been snapped up by one of the other staffers who nabbed every stray piece of music before he knew it had come in. He slipped the case into his backpack like he was stealing jewelry, and brought it back to his apartment. At last Zan Williams had come out of retirement. The name change meant nothing—how could such a musical genius be anything but true to his art, still pertinent, more than ever, to popular song? Mars shut the window in his single room and turned the volume high. He parked himself in front of the speakers to listen and revel in the sound, and then he'd write a review that would make it clear to the neophytes he was forced to share column inches with what music could be— what it should be.

But two bars in he knew it was not music, but some kind of Islamic sermon, blatant proselytizing, the musical equivalent of televangelism. *The truth's not open to debate / and when you die / you won't get by on a lie / and your repentance will be too late.* This wasn't even Christian rock, borrowing chords and riffs from other genres, and altering the words to moralize. It was just a man, a cappella at times, at others accompanied by a simple drum and flute. Where was the intellect, the sophistication that had inspired him before? These tracks weren't even songs, but poems— probably lifted from scripture. Why not just include a Quran instead of a lyric sheet with each CD?

Even stoned the music did nothing for him. This was someone pretending to be Zan Williams, trying to cash in on the artist people remembered. And he sang of peace, but where was the peace in the religion he'd adopted? Jihadist atrocities had become more and more common, but every time he had a chance to recant his conversion, Williams stood by Islam, instead of denouncing it and coming back to his roots.

Mars took the CD out of the player and flung it against the wall. "Give us back our Alexander Williams!"

He obsessed over it for a week, and then he knew what he had to do. But the magazine's publisher said he simply couldn't, wouldn't shell out that kind of money to send him across the Atlantic for the uncertain return of a story about a forgotten folk-rock hippie. "What the fuck, Mars?" the publisher said. "Dude's old enough to be a member of AARP."

Mars almost hit him then. This kid, this pretender would have been bussing tables if it weren't for his father's money. Instead he called the shots, and the magazine profiled the popular noise of the street. It dismissed rock, relegating it to a column called "Retro Stars with Johnny Mars," buried in the back pages alongside ads for personal trainers, dog walkers, credit repair and call-girl services. If it hadn't been for Mars's long-ago friendship with the publisher's father, he wouldn't even have that.

Why didn't the kid get it? Why didn't the world get it? Why, he wondered, didn't Zan Williams get it? But if the public cared, had remained devoted to the music and its message, he wouldn't be working for a throwaway named Pink Toaster instead of a magazine with influence.

He would pay for the trip himself. It was too important not to. He booked a flight on a discount carrier, and endured a sleepless overnighter jammed into a middle seat. He found lodging in an old guidebook he'd kept since his college days—one of London's less-than-fashionable back street hotels—a place called the Georgian House, with accommodations that appeared to date from the Blitz: an army cot, a school kid's wooden chair and a dilapidated armoire whose door opened into the light fixture that dangled from the ceiling, swinging it like a pendulum every time he changed clothes. There was space in this room for him and his suitcase, and that was all. At night he sat in a chair in the corner and listened over and over to one of the old songs from the seventies that was included, for whatever reason, on the CD. An anomaly perhaps, or maybe there was an open track and nothing else to fill it, but it was good to hear Williams's voice recreating this treasure again, good to be transported back to a time when it seemed Mars's future would be an idyllic mix of song and commentary, and respect from his peers.

Those old LP cuts, had, for a time, been his life's soundtrack—he quoted Williams's lyrics in English Lit essays; they played on a second-hand turntable when he lost his virginity with a girl from his Sociology class, whom he seduced with sangria and his scratchy harmony to Zan's singing. He was sure then, he was in love—with the girl, with the sound, with life.

He forced himself to listen to the rest of the CD again through ear buds, making notes about the voice, the instruments, and in particular, the lyrics. At last Ali's intent became clear. The next morning he went to a coffee shop and spent hours online, doing what he had to do, gathering the evidence he needed to indict his former idol.

And with Ali nattering on about concert venues, and the audience drinking it all in, Mars knows the time is right to expose this fraud for what he is. He stands again. He sees the guard coming for him, and knows there will be others, and that this time they will be physical. The heat of the room envelopes him once more. His breathing quickens and he feels his skin burning. The hall begins to spin around him, and for a moment he forgets in which direction the stage sits. But he will not be silenced. He bellows above the singer's words. "You say your religion is about peace, but all over the world it brings violence and war. It murders innocent people. How can your music defend that?"

The man on the dais next to Ali rises and places his fists on the table. He leans forward as if preparing to berate the critic, but the singer puts a hand over his. The producer sits down, and Ali speaks. "You can say that Islam supports violence, just as you can say that many other religions support violence. History is filled with examples. In every faith, there are some who believe violence is the answer. I do not. We could debate this all day, but please, we are here to talk about the music."

Mars has the contradiction he was hoping for, and pulls printouts of newspaper clippings from his back pocket. For a second he pauses—sees himself as Judas. No! It was Zan Williams who betrayed us! He unfolds the papers and holds them far enough away so his tired eyes can focus. A bead of sweat runs from his forehead, down his cheek, like a tear. He reads, "When Islamic terrorists held a group of American workers hostage and beheaded one of them in 1991, you were asked what you thought of the crisis. You said, and I quote, 'The death is regrettable, but necessary. It is important to focus the world's attention on the plight of our people.'" He shakes the paper and repeats, "Necessary!"

The guards reach Mars and each one takes an arm. He struggles against them to continue reading, but the papers fall to the floor and under his seat.

Ali puts his hand to his chin, mimicking the thoughtful portrait behind him.

The producer stands. "This is old news," he says. "We're not here to talk about what happened so many years ago."

IV: The most excellent Jihad is that for the conquest of self
—Bukhari hadith

Ali watches as the man undulates like a giant worm in the grasp of the guards, unable to free himself. He sees his reddening face, the locked muscles of his neck. The producer leans over and asks, "What is this one so mad about?" Ali senses it is not anger, but pain. He holds out a hand as though to heal him, and tells the guards to let him go. They release the man, but station themselves at the ends of the row. The producer signals an aide over and tells her to call the police.

Ali says, "No. I don't think we need to go that far. Besides, how would it look in the media? They'll say I wouldn't face questions about my past."

"Then what do you want to do?"

"I'll talk to him." He looks out to the back row and addresses the man. "Mister…"

"…Mars," the man finishes. A few people in the crowd snicker. Someone to the side muffles a bigger laugh. "It's short for Marsden."

"You know a great deal about me. To be honest, I don't recall saying that. I do remember it was a very difficult time for many people. But if I did say it, then I am sure God has forgiven my discretion. I pray that others can find it in themselves to forgive as well."

"Let us rejoice in the music," the producer says, "and forget the differences of the past. They will get us nowhere."

But Ali does remember those words. The comments replay in his conscience as he lies to the crowd. What else could he have done? Muslims were upset over persecution by westerners. A few even protested in the streets of London. The local mullahs urged him to speak in defense of Islam, and when he agreed to go to the media on their behalf, they pressured him to take a hard line. It was not something he'd planned to say. He wished he could somehow take it back. Now he'd hoped the years would be enough to bury the comment, but there is always someone digging.

Ali looks into the faces of the crowd. They want more. They always do. When he was touring they didn't just expect him to address their concerns, they wanted him to tell them how to think about the issues, even to decide which issues were worth discussing. It hasn't changed, he sees. Why won't they let him be just a singer?

Now this man, this Mars, is trying to affix the mantle of all Islam on his shoulders; trying, like his fans once did, to anoint him as its leader. Ali feels an urge to lecture them on the irony of why he'd converted to Islam. It had appealed so much because it wanted him as a follower—it did not ask him to lead. God simply reached out His hand and pulled him in.

*

Zan Williams floated ten thousand feet above the ground. His first solo parachute jump, in cloudless, perfect weather. For a few seconds he surfed the wind, scanning endless vistas over southern California farmland, the rush of air cleansing his mind, its roar exiling his troubles. It was as dreamlike as his days on drugs, and he stretched his body wide to experience it completely. But when he pulled on the cord to open the chute, nothing happened. He twisted from fear, but managed to reach the reserve cord, and congratulated himself for remaining composed enough to remember the emergency procedure. He pulled. But again, the chute didn't respond.

He plunged into panic—he couldn't think—began to claw at the pack on his back, trying to rip it apart to free the jammed chute, but he could barely touch it. He kicked at the air, convulsed his body as he watched the stunning scene below become a passage to hell. Seconds remained. He screamed and begged, calling on a God he had not spoken to since childhood. "God! God! Please save me! I'll be yours." And at last he began to cry, his tears burning his eyes under the goggles. He shut them so he wouldn't see the earth rushing up. It was what God had been waiting for. The reserve chute somehow worked its way out of the pack and caught the air. Just a few hundred feet off the ground it jerked Zan Williams higher, dislocating his shoulder in the process, but then cradling him back to a field of alfalfa, as though carried in God's palm.

He had made a promise, and for once he would keep it. It was clear to him that this was a sign. He turned to the Bible, to the Catholicism of his youth, searching for a path by which he might fulfill his pledge. But in the months that followed he did not find the answers. So much was ambivalent. So many passages had been perverted by people seeking to manipulate the meanings. He wanted to serve, but the way was unclear, perplexing, ambiguous. Faith beckoned, yet evaded him.

Then his brother, Steven, delivered the solution in the form of the Quran. "Read this," he said, "and you'll know the truth." And in that text the doubt and questions were eliminated. In the Quran there was no room for uncertainty—the way to Allah was as simple and beautiful as a flower turning its face to the sun. Zan Williams understood why he was placed in such peril in the sky; he knew and accepted his destiny, and prepared a statement for the public.

But since then it had been a struggle—despite what he said publicly, he had missed making music for a long time. At first his joy over discovering Islam was enough to fill the void, but in less than a year the passion faded. The rigidity of study and prayer bored him—he no longer felt God flowing into him. Instead he felt shackled to a life of obligation, structured to keep him from questioning authority. How he missed the old debates about the nature of things.

The emptiness left him melancholy. He began to crave the melodies he'd written. His old songs played in his head, like an orchestra, far away, offering him a way to fill the silent hours of contemplation that were supposed to be reserved for Allah. Even during Salat he heard the music trying to drown out the recitative. His fingers itched to touch the strings of his guitars, to feel the cool of piano keys. He eventually had to sell all the instruments—get them out of the house—to resist their temptations.

He consulted with local clerics to seek a solution. He didn't want to give up either world. Why did one have to win out over the other? Their only advice was to pray even harder and ask for Allah's help.

That calmed him for a few months. But at a charity event he ran into a woman he had known from his former record company, and another old itch afflicted him. The affair with her lasted two years, and was followed by others, all with women outside his religion. Even as he debates Mars he pauses for a second to think about a rendezvous he has planned for later, after the dinner that is to follow the conference, with a young staff member at the ad firm for the new CD. The hypocrisy of it all has long since ceased to matter.

At least his constant pressure persuaded the scholars to find an interpretation of scripture that allows him to go back to singing and composing. Finally, they ruled that if the music were considered to be in the service of God, it would be permitted. But now even that is not enough.

"I hope, Mister Marsden, that I've answered your question," Ali says. "Yes, I've made some mistakes. We all have, I'd guess. But I certainly don't want the people here to get the impression I'm some kind of violent fanatic. I'm a bit too old and mellow for that kind of thing." Enough people in the audience laugh at the joke to make Ali smile. They are still with him.

"Now," he adds, "I really must insist you hold the rest of your questions for the time allotted." The guards turn towards Mars. They seem to be relishing a chance to do their jobs.

V: I hold fast my righteousness and will not let it go—Job 27:6

He's getting away with it. Ali hasn't answered the question at all, not to Mars's satisfaction, and the crowd is ignoring the issue, preferring, as they always do, to sit back and let someone else take the risks. He wants to continue the inquiry, to push harder, but he won't be able to say much before the guards are on him. He will have to wait for the right moment. If he doesn't find a way to expose this fraud, another generation might be subjected to the lie that is Zan Williams.

Mars sits back down and reaches under the seat for the printouts. He takes out the notepad again, burying his head in it in hopes the guards will be placated and shift their attention elsewhere. For now, he plans to continue the fight in print—in his column. He composes passages. He will polish them tonight in the room and send the article back to the states in the morning. He'll start with how Zan Williams sold out his fans thirty years ago, and how Ahmed Ali is trying to sell them out again by passing off an album of prayers and propaganda as music. Don't believe it, he writes. Like me, you may have once been a fan and believed his lyrics were honest, that his music promoted love and tolerance. But you can't trust him anymore! He has been swallowed up by radical Muslims—our enemies—and now he does their bidding, trying to convince us we have nothing to fear. Mars flexes his hand to stop it from shaking.

That's a good start. He'll demand the kid run the column in the front of the magazine, with a refer on the cover, instead of lost among the detritus of the back pages. If he doesn't, Mars will take it to larger, more prestigious publications, until one of them buys the story. Maybe he should go to them to begin with, rather than waste his efforts on a free weekly.

The press conference goes on around him. Ali finishes discussing the album and the tour, and asks for a guitar so he can perform one of the cuts from the CD—an impromptu performance to the delight of the audience. But Mars isn't listening. He is on his third page, writing about the contradictions that pervade every aspect of Zan Williams's life: he was a hedonist, then a spiritualist; now a terrorist, and he will use his celebrity to undermine the world that gave him fame. He says his is a religion of peace, but when he was put on the spot, he supported violence against innocents—Mars has the quotes to prove it, no matter what Ali says now.

He retrieves the second printout and studies it for a few seconds. Another drop falls from his eye to the paper. This is a copy of Ali's letter to the media after terrorists flew planes into the World Trade Center. Ali played it safe, of course, saying the event was "a tragedy," but what did he really think? Most of the letter was a defense of his religion—don't hate Muslims because of what happened—just a few lines were concerned with the actual atrocity. There was no real remorse.

Mars writes with a violence of his own now, pressing his pen into the notepad so hard it tears through to the next page. He had watched on television as the second jet exploded into the side of the South Tower.

Mars wipes away the moisture that makes it difficult to see. He feels the same nausea as he did on that day. He rises again. His hands and knees will not keep still. Ali is in the middle of his song; the audience is rapt. Mars stretches his eyes as wide as they will go. He shouts, "Tell us about the World Trade Center! Tell us how your religion of peace wasn't responsible for that!"

The guards take hold of him almost immediately and drag him towards the side aisle. He keeps on screaming, "You fraud! It's all a lie, isn't it?" They grasp him tighter and one of them pulls his arms behind his back as though he is going to handcuff him. Mars starts to shout again, but the other guard slaps a hand over his mouth. He kicks the second man in the shin and the big guard winces. They take him through a side door and into a service hallway, where more CDs and press packages are stacked on a folding table. When the door bangs shut the second guard shoulders Mars against the wall and pounds a fist like a sledgehammer into his stomach. Mars clutches his midsection and goes limp, spilling the display as he collapses into the lotus position on the floor. He looks down to see Ali peering up from the covers of a half dozen jewel cases, each face with the same placid smile, the same vacant eyes. It takes him a couple of minutes to recover, and when he does he picks one of the CDs up and holds it at arm's length, and feels the anger within him succumb to an icy cold.

VI: Kindness is a mark of faith—Muslim hadith

The crowd turns to watch the commotion. Some of them gasp; a few, recognizing the man from his previous disturbances, begin to laugh. But several of the reporters call for Ali to answer questions about the remarks he made after the attack. He rests his guitar on the floor and stands. "We should be concerned for that man. He is troubled," he says. The outburst brings the images of that day in New York back to Ali, but it is too painful a memory to consider for very long. The statement he released had been the proper response—a message of tolerance and healing offered to a world in pain. It was what had been expected of him.

It's pointless to go on singing. Ali leaves the guitar and stands at the microphone. "I apologize, but I think it's best if we end the press conference here. I know I promised to take your questions, but in light of the disturbances… I'd like to get some rest. I hope you understand."

"Do you know that man?" a reporter shouts. Others want to know about his past statements, about his conversion to Islam in the first place. Two reporters run up the aisle to the emergency exit and try to locate Mars, but one of the guards comes out and blocks the doors. Ali signals to the rest that he won't cooperate. "I'm too tired," he says. "This is not the right time." The producer comes over and puts his arm around Ali, and leads him off stage, telling him over and over that he has done the right thing.

"I want to go home," Ali says. "I have to think about whether I'll make it to the dinner later." But if he doesn't, it will be impossible to slip away for his affair with the young staffer afterwards. She is a recent university graduate, blond and lean, all of maybe twenty-three. She knows nothing about his past in America, nothing about the things he's said in public. She knows there had been a Trade Center in the states, and that it had been destroyed, but other than that she is not clear on the details, not sure who was responsible and why they did it.

Ali's aides accompany him towards the front of the building, where his limo waits. He stops the procession. "No. Find another way out of here. The reporters are probably hanging around the entrance, and I don't want to have to face their questions right now." A member of the building's security crew says he knows a way, and he leads the group into a maze of hallways that ring the auditorium. An aide calls and has the car drive around to the back.

As they turn into a dim passage at the rear, they come across Mars, sitting on the floor, strings of hair matted to his forehead, still recovering from his encounter with the guards. One of the big men stands over him. Several copies of Moon and Star are scattered on the linoleum, some still in their cellophane wrappers, others unsealed for the display. Mars holds one of the disks by the edges with the thumb and fingers of one hand, pressing his forefinger near the center, bending the glossy plastic into a crescent.

"He won't bother you now," the guard says to Ali. "I'll make sure of that."

"Are you all right, sir?" Ali asks.

Mars doesn't answer.

"The police should be here any minute and we'll have him out of your way."

Ali stops in front of the man and looks down, as though studying the past.

"Leave him, Ahmed," the producer says. "There's nothing you can do for him."

"I don't want him charged."

"What?"

"After we leave, just let him go. Tell the police it was a misunderstanding."

"Are you certain?"

"Please… don't argue with me."

Ali stands, waiting. He does not expect an apology or a thank you, but he wants the man to speak, if only to rant about the wrongs he had perceived over the years, and compare him to the man he used to be, or to threaten to haunt him, haunt his conscience, for the rest of his life. He wants to hear something from him, rather than be left alone with thoughts and memories, with all the people whom he knows can never understand.

But Mars only stares at the disk in his hand, muttering, grimacing as though carrying on a debate in his head. He keeps pressing the CD back onto itself, his hand trembling wildly, until it cracks in half, the sound reverberating off the walls like a gunshot. The pieces glance off Mars's leg and rattle against the floor, and lay there with the jagged cuts facing each other. "A broken promise," he says. The producer and another aide take Ali by the shoulders and usher him away.

At the door to the back of the hall Ali steps through, then pauses before continuing on to the black car, where an immaculate driver in a cap with a patent leather bill smiles and waits, holding the door for him. Beyond the driver and the car are the backs of nearby buildings, defiled with graffiti, some of it profane and targeted at Muslims. He looks over the structures into the London afternoon, a typically gray sky overlaying the blue. He remembers that he hasn't seen the sun for a long time. It seems as though to see it is not so much a right as a privilege.

Minutiae (Author's Notes)

The Face Maker

I've always been a lover of history, and no period fascinates me more than the World War I era, mostly because of the immense changes in technology and government that occurred at that time, and how they influenced the century to come. This was the apex of the Industrial Revolution and scientific curiosity, two compatible, yet opposing tracks that allowed for the development of the first weapons of mass destruction, yet also implanted in the common man the idea that s/he was something more than just a disposable tool who worked for the benefit of the monarchy and upper classes. During the course of the war (1914-1918), four major European monarchies were overthrown: Russia, Germany, Austria-Hungary and the Ottoman Empire (Turkey); other nations, such as Spain, Italy, Bulgaria and Romania, toppled their monarchies in the decades following.

My interest in this time was largely kindled by a documentary series that aired on PBS back in the 1990s called "The Great War: and the Shaping of the Twentieth Century," produced by Jay Winter and Blaine Bagett. This was simply the best documentary

I've ever seen. Unfortunately, it's still not available on DVD, much to the disappointment of its many fans. The story of the Face Maker was inspired by a segment in the series that showed perhaps the most human cost of the conflict, men who'd lost their faces to modern weaponry. Despite other advancements in medicine, plastic surgery was virtually nonexistent at the time. So to treat these disfigured men, artists were called in to create façades to cover what the war had stolen, helping restore a human face to the grotesqueries imposed by the hatreds that ignited the war, and reminding the world that compassion and empathy still had a place in society.

The Killer of the Writer

I am often fascinated and frustrated by how popular opinion and sales goals influence the decisions of large publishing companies. Like television and movies, it's the taste of the mass market, as unsophisticated as it may be, that drives the industry and forces most truly gifted writers to exist on the margins, misunderstood and largely underappreciated. How many potentially great writers are never allowed to participate in the literary conversation because their passion can't outlast years of rejection and the need to make a living? The premise behind "Killer," is exactly what it appears to be—a nobody with talent trying to understand why a hack like Lazlo became famous. It's primarily a commentary on our infatuation with celebrity, and how that celebrity tends to dictate our standards for genius, rather than vice versa. The magical realism that Pagan writes, by the way, represents the only path he sees still available to him, both on a literary and a personal level. Such a choice confronts many excellent writers today—either they give themselves over to cheap thrillers and vampire sagas or remain in literature's desert, because the publishing business's hyper-emphasis on self-promotion dooms the industry to producing work by those with the loudest and most self-centered voices.

Living in Dark Houses

As children, we tend not to question our family and affiliations—the places in which we grew up are sanctified. But as we mature, sometimes we understand that those places were not as nurturing as we were told to believe. When I was growing up in the suburbs of Long Island I knew no other culture—the hatreds and bullying I endured throughout my school years were the norm, and if anyone had brought that torture on, it was I.

I had long forgotten about an incident that happened on my street when I was about twelve: an older boy—maybe sixteen—took a .22 rifle and shot his father. (He survived.) In those days such matters were left to the family, and so the media frenzy one might expect today was limited to a few lines in the local paper. The rest of the neighborhood were left to their imaginations as to why it happened. But decades later I was reminded of the incident, and by extension, the darkness of my childhood. What kind of place could foster and accept such violence? Having since lived in a dozen other places around the country I've come to see the suburbs of my childhood as a more confining place—both physically and spiritually—than I was earlier able to admit. And I've learned there are many other such places in which I might have grown up. This has helped me to be at least a little more open to other people and other cultures, although I'm still working on it. The outside, the other side, is rarely as evil as we make it out to be.

The Sting of the Glove

Boxing is one of the more primitive arts remaining in our culture, and makes for an excellent backdrop against which to analyze our primitive urges. This story came from a prompt in one of my writers' groups, and immediately led to an examination of our baser instincts and how they tend to muck up our ability to relate to each other. Lust and pride battle against love and loyalty.

That kind of fight is not easy to win, mostly because it's never over. Eddie Sharkey, like Brando's Terry Malloy in "On the Waterfront," could have been a contender, could have been somebody, but he falls short, both in the ring and outside it.

Nixon in State

As a high school student during the Watergate hearings I would sit in my car in the school parking lot and listen to the proceedings. I may not have known exactly what it all meant, but I knew it was important. Years later I stood in that line in Yorba Linda waiting for a glimpse of the president lying in state (the rest of the story, though, is fiction). Perhaps no other public figure in our history so exemplified the changes in our cultural values, from a nation of implicit trust in our leaders to one of almost complete mistrust, from a respect for privacy to an utter disregard for it. Nixon was a good president and a paranoid man, but mostly he was the wrong man to be in office during the media's rise to prominence. The combination of his warped sense of importance, his egomaniacal devotion to his perceived place in history, and the media's growing preoccupation with what happens behind the scenes made for the perfect storm of news coverage. Ever since, it seems, the public has been unwilling to trust, which leads to an unwillingness to compromise. And that, practiced via gerrymandering, extremism and the breakdown of public education (among many other ills), leads to our current political system, in which sincere men and women find it virtually impossible to pass meaningful legislation. To look at Nixon is, in some ways, to look at ourselves, and what we've become. My story is intended to examine that through a smaller lens, one of personal relationships that essentially mirror those corrupted values. Are we better off seeking ultimate truths about every person, every event? I hope the story helps the reader examine that question.

The final three stories in this collection were not published, mostly because (I hope) I haven't sent them out much. It's been difficult to find journals that would be good fits for them, although I hope that doesn't mean they're not decent stories.

Caging the Butterfly

A simple idea of a May-December romance turned into pure psychological horror. Sometimes it's important for a writer to wonder just how far a person will go to exact revenge. How deep is the obsession? This story has no tie to me personally, and therefore it was probably the most fun I've ever had writing—never mind moral values or personal reflection, just let the old rich guy manipulate everyone he knows. Kind of like real life in that respect.

Excerpts from the Diary of the Last Roman Emperor

The story of Romulus Augustulus is one of the more fascinating tales from history. There is a human infatuation with the end of great things, and that is what inspired me to wonder about the last emperor of the Roman Empire (we're talking Rome here, not Constantinople). Certainly Augustulus wasn't the reason for the empire's dissolution, but being the last in that thousand-year history sets him up as a scapegoat, one of history's biggest losers. When I started the research into this story I was completely hooked. The facts of his life were perfect for fiction, and I'm certainly not the first writer to figure that out—there have been a play, a movie and even a comic book based on Augustulus's life. As in most cases when leadership is thrust upon someone completely unprepared, it's those around him who take control, and the worst possible outcomes are usually the ones that occur.

What We Choose to Remember

Long before I dedicated myself to writing I had pondered the meaning of the decades in which I grew up. The 1960s were a time of radically changing views about our country and our culture—a new generation questioned everything that had come before. I was too young to participate in the chaos and exhilaration of those days, but the tone they set, and the liberal education I received, became part of the foundation of my adult beliefs. But the attitudes of those days lasted only a short time. By the late 1970s the country was already back in the grip of conformity, and we've never returned (except in small cultural pockets) to the days of broad social conscience. So I have often wondered about the nature of counterculture, whether it represents an awakening to greater ideals, or is essentially a passing fad, gaining followers because it's popular rather than right, and eventually giving way to the next big thing. I think no other example better illustrates the questions surrounding this time and issues than the career of Cat Stevens, on which this fiction is based. He was one of my favorite performers of the 1970s, and then he disappeared—gave up his singing and composing to follow Islam, way before it was common to do so. I felt, and still believe, that Stevens (now Yusuf Islam) wrestled with the same issues about truth and fame that are represented in the story, although the character Zan Williams, with his insincerities and philandering, is in no way intended to be Stevens/Islam himself—those aspects were added to act as a metaphor for the hypocrisy and rationalizations that often accompany fame. Then there's Johnny Mars, who like me, wonders why it had to change. He gives voice to the questions that have intrigued me about this time, although he's far more intractable about his inquiries than I. His representation in the story as a total loser is an exaggeration of those people who can't let go of a cherished past, and because they can't integrate society's inevitable changes, allow themselves to become the outcasts of the present.

One of the interesting criticisms of this story, from both writer friends and editors, has been the inclusion of the World Trade

Center attack in 2001. People have said this aspect lessened their appreciation of the story, as though they felt the event has already been examined so thoroughly they can't handle one more reference to it. But my opinion is just the opposite—we're far from done with it, nor should we be. This single event crystallized decades of western influence in the Middle East and the animosities that had been building. And Yusuf Islam was asked to speak on behalf of the Muslim community in the aftermath of the atrocity, so it felt natural to extend the story to include some rationale that would allow Mars to take his questions from mere inquiries into obsessions.

- JP

About the Author

Joe Ponepinto spent the first half of his life in a variety of mercenary pursuits. To make up for it, he now writes, edits or teaches every day. He has worked as the Book Review Editor for *The Los Angeles Review*, and Co-Editor of *Delphi Quarterly*, an online journal featuring artist interviews. His short stories have been published in many literary journals. Joe was a journalist, political speechwriter and business owner before turning to writing full time in 2006. A New York native, he spent 28 years in LA, and currently lives in Michigan with his wife, Dona, and Henry, the coffee drinking dog. His blog, *The Saturday Morning Post*, has thousands of followers and can be found at http://joeponepinto.com. To send questions about the stories in this book, requests for interviews, readings or other appearances, email him at jpon@thirdreader.com.

Acknowledgments

A writer's life is a lonely one by choice, made up of days spent in the slow process of creation, and often spiced only with criticism and rejection. So I owe a debt of gratitude to two groups of writers whose encouragement has kept me going, and whose influence has helped shape my craft to this point. The first group includes colleagues from the Northwest Institute for Literary Arts in Coupeville, Washington. Bruce Holland Rogers, Kathleen Alcalá, Wayne Ude, Carolyne Wright, Ana Maria Spagna, Larry Cheek and one of the great American poets, David Wagoner, have all provided guidance and inspiration. I'm especially indebted to Kelly Davio, Kobbie Alamo and Stephanie Barbé Hammer, who have consistently expressed belief in my writing when it seems no one else has.

The second group is made up of local writers in the Detroit area. My good friends Stewart Sternberg, Jon Zech and Christine Purcell—all fine writers themselves—have been there through the years, sometimes sharing my frustrations over the cronyism and unfairness of the publishing business, and sometimes just offering a much-needed laugh.

A special note of thanks and love to my beautiful wife, Dona, whose willingness to support this obsession of mine, despite the many hours when I made myself both physically and emotionally unavailable, made this book possible.

Finally, a quick bark out to Henry, alias the coffee drinkin' dog, who has never written a thing, but has inspired many a blog post and short story, and who will always be more popular than I am on the internet. Here's to my little buddy.

Made in the USA
Charleston, SC
24 August 2013